Bride by Midnight

Linda Winstead Jones

Copyright © 2013 by Linda Winstead Jones.
Published by Linda Winstead Jones

Print Edition
ISBN: 978-0615783277

All rights reserved under International and Pan-American Copyright Conventions.

Cover design by Elizabeth Wallace
http://designwithin.carbonmade.com/

Print Design by A Thirsty Mind
http://www.athirstymind.com

Prologue

Columbyana, the eighth year of the reign of Emperor Nechtyn Jahn Calcus Sadwyn Beckyt

"You must be a wife well and true, a wife in all ways before your twenty-third birthday, or you will live your life alone."

Standing on the side of the narrow road that snaked through the forest Lyssa stared, wide-eyed, at the crone who delivered the ominous message in a voice that cracked ever so slightly. Alone? Her? Impossible! She had just recently celebrated her fifteenth birthday, and already her father had received offers for her hand. Some of the offers were unsuitable, as the men in question were either too old or too poor or too ugly—not that she was unreasonably demanding—but there were a few intriguing possibilities. And if those who had already expressed an interest in taking her as a wife did not suit after further inspection, there would be others in the years to come. She would certainly be a wife long before she reached the age of twenty-three. As for "well and true?" "In all ways?" What did that mean, exactly? One was a wife or else one was not.

Lyssa smiled tightly, determined to be polite even though the woman who had delivered the portent was not well-acquainted with personal hygiene or acceptable manners. She glanced down and brushed a nonexistent speck of dirt from the sleeve of her linen blouse, just so she would have a respite from looking into the old woman's intense eyes. When Lyssa and her father had met the poor soul on the road early on the previous evening, she'd seemed to be helpless and lost, and desperately in need of food. She looked as if she'd been broken in half and repaired improperly, canting to one side and walking as if she might tip over at any moment. She'd said her name was Vellance, and she had gratefully accepted food and water, and a ride in the wagon. Last night she'd settled down to sleep a respectable distance from Lyssa and her father, and she *had* slept. Lyssa knew because the woman had rattled the leaves of the trees around them with her snoring.

The witch's clothing—yes, surely the hag was a witch, why else would she be shooting daggers with her narrowed eyes and speaking of Lyssa's future as if she knew what was to come?—was black and loose and dirty, ripped and ill-repaired in several places. The filthy hem dragged the ground occasionally, but not always, hiding her bare feet and disturbingly gnarled toenails. The old woman's hair was a tangled gray and brown-streaked mess, and a number of teeth were missing. Now and then the hag's words whistled through the unfortunate gaps.

Many travelers would have passed her by without a second glance, but Cyrus Tempest, Lyssa's father, was an extraordinarily kind man who was always willing to help a person in need. Even one who looked like she might have stepped out of a child's nightmare.

He hadn't known the old woman would scare the breath out of his only child.

"You don't believe me," Vellance said in a lowered voice.

Lyssa smoothed a slight wrinkle from her rose colored skirt and then glanced toward the stream, where her father was collecting water for the three of them. The forest thinned a bit along this part of the road; the shadows were less worrisome; the sunlight broke through and shone down here and there. Spring was Lyssa's favorite season. The air was neither hot nor cold, and flowers bloomed all around. Butterflies flitted about in abundance, white and yellow and blue. Vellance's presence was ruining what should have been a perfectly lovely day!

It would be unkind to spurn the old woman who was so obviously in need, but at that moment Lyssa would have given almost anything to see the witch far, far away. She should have stayed home with her stepmother instead of insisting on making the trip to the seaside market with her father. The war with the Isen Demon was eight years behind them, and despite the occasional uproar and hysteria over the existence of an unknown number of the demon's children—daughters all, children still—the roads were safe. Well, as safe as they could be. One heard the infrequent tale of robbery, and on rare occasion there might be a mysterious disappearance, but those tales were rare, and she did know better than to believe *everything* she heard.

If Lyssa did believe everything she heard, she might be more worried about half-demon little girls of seven and eight years old who might or might not possess unnatural powers inherited from their sire. There were whispers about different sorts of demon daughters and the magic they wielded. Fire-starters; those whose wishes came true; shape shifters; children who could touch the minds of others. Did they use their powers for good or for evil? To kill or to save? Truth be told, there were more stories of demon spawn who were perfectly ordinary little girls than…otherwise. And until she saw *otherwise* for herself, she wasn't going to worry.

Not when there were real problems to worry about. Like Vellance.

Maybe she should have stayed home, but she so loved the sea. She loved the smell, the sight of the endless waves, and the way the ships moved upon those waves. Traveling with her father had seemed an appropriate and relatively small risk when compared to the reward of reaching the seaside.

This unpleasant experience would teach her to listen to her stepmother, who had tried to convince Lyssa to stay at home. Adventures were not meant for everyone. They certainly were not to Lyssa Tempest's tastes. Her plans, her dreams, were ordinary. She knew what she wanted: a kind husband; a simple home of her own. Babies. And all of it long before she reached the ripe old age of twenty-three.

"It's not that I don't believe you." Lyssa once again worked up the nerve to look Vellance in the eye, which was more difficult than she liked. Still, she tried to keep her tone sweet, because she had been taught to be respectful of her elders. God knows, Vellance was about as *elder* as one got. "It's just that I plan to be married no later than the age of eighteen. There have already been offers, and though I would like to wait a couple of years and study all my options carefully before I choose a husband, I certainly won't wait until I'm so old as twenty-three."

The witch smiled. Lyssa suppressed a shudder. "Plans have a way of going awry, child. I'm proof of that fact. Once I was pretty, like you, and I had opportunities such as yours. Men begged for my affections. Women were jealous of my lustrous hair and flawless skin. When your beauty fades—and it *will* fade, I assure you—what will become of your grand plans?"

"My plans are not grand at all," Lyssa argued without heat, trying—and failing—to picture the witch before her as an attractive young woman. "I'll marry a nice man, have children, and keep a home as my stepmother does. As I always wished for brothers and sisters, I would like to have a large family. I suppose we will live in Arthes, so I can be close to my father, but if my husband's livelihood takes us elsewhere, then I will endure the separation, as many wives must. All in all, I intend to live a perfectly ordinary life."

"Whether you marry or not, your life will not be ordinary. You have magic in your blood, girl. It sleeps, but it will not sleep forever," the witch said in a voice that was simultaneously confident and gloomy—and annoyingly smug. Vellance turned her dark eyes toward the creek, where Lyssa's father was finishing up his task and stretching tired bones.

Lyssa stood tall—not an easy feat, given that she was far from it—and brushed back a wayward strand of hair. Anxious, she rocked up onto her toes and back down again. What if the witch really did possess some power that offered a glimpse of the future? Lyssa was quite sure no magic slept within her. After all, magic was an inherited trait, and her parents were perfectly normal people. Her father was a shop keeper, and her mother had been the daughter of a farmer. Though Lyssa did not remember the woman who'd given birth to her, her father's stories of the wife he'd lost long ago were sweet and melancholy and ordinary. There had been no mention of magic.

Lyssa didn't think for a moment that she would have any trouble finding a husband when the time came. Though she wasn't a great beauty, she was hardly a troll. Her hair wasn't a brilliant gold, as she'd been told her mother's had been, but was instead her father's more ordinary brown. At least there was plenty of it, and it waved nicely when she wore it down. Her eyes were an odd shade of green, not her mother's blue or her father's brown, but they were nicely shaped. Maybe her chin was a little too pointed, but as her father had said time and again, that sharpness gave her face character.

Vellance must be wrong. Still…Lyssa found herself growing more and more curious. Her insatiable curiosity was a trait her father had bemoaned for as long as she could remember. Who wouldn't wonder if there might not be a touch of truth in the words of an old witch who seemed so certain that she knew details of the years ahead? Just a touch, though. At that moment Lyssa decided that there was no reason why she could not *choose* which portents to accept and which ones to dismiss.

"If you know so much about the future, *my* future, why don't you just tell me who I'm supposed to marry, and when?" If there was knowledge to be had, why shouldn't she take advantage of it? "The knowing will save me a lot of trouble. I rather like Atman Rybar. He's very handsome and will likely continue his father's fabric trade, which would keep us in Arthes, but sometimes he seems vain and distracted and, well, not particularly bright." She sighed. Besides, it could be argued that he was prettier than she was. "Tanni Onund is much smarter than Atman, but he's also rather dull." Her words were tumbling over one another, but she didn't want to give the witch a chance to speak again unless she was going to offer accurate and *pleasant* information. "Not that I'm looking for excitement in a husband, mind you." But there was a lot of room between *dull* and *exciting*. "Then there's—"

"It doesn't work that way," the witch said sharply. She was apparently unwilling to wait for Lyssa to finish before she had her say. "Your life is not laid before me like a map of the Southern Province, with well marked roads that lead to your destination and clearly marked cliffs to avoid. No, your life lies off the road, off the map. You must choose the way." Her eyes narrowed. "Choose wisely and your life will be blessed. Choose poorly and you will spend all your long years alone. Perhaps you will wander through this very forest, as I wander, hoping for strangers to offer sustenance and companionship." Her eyes seemed to spark, as if lightning struck there. "Trust me when I tell you, you do not want to live your life as I do."

Those words had more impact than anything else the witch had said since she'd begun traveling with Lyssa and her father. To be alone, to have no one to turn to in good times or in bad…To perhaps end up wandering the road in her old age, crooked and mostly toothless, scaring young women with ridiculous portents…

Suddenly she could actually see herself doing exactly that, the scene forming so sharply in her mind it was as if the world around her had changed. Everything in her recoiled, and reality snapped back into place.

Lyssa shook off the dark sensations that had so briefly whipped through her. She was young, passably pretty, kind, and sought after. While she was far from being a fine lady, her father was a well-respected and successful merchant. She would not be alone, not ever. She would have her father and a caring stepmother until she married, and when the time came to choose a husband, she would have several from whom to pick. By the time she was twenty-three she would have a loving husband who would dote upon her the way her father doted on Sinmora, and they would have at least two or three children.

Alone?

Never.

Vellance leaned closer and lowered her voice. "Perhaps I should speak more plainly." She held up a gnarled finger. "By the age of twenty-three you must be a proper wife, well-bedded and properly claimed, one half of a couple. If you take heed and ensure the path you take is the right one, all will be well.

"But if you ignore my warning you will have no one, and your powers will shift to darkness. The dark part of this world wants you, Lyssa. The darkness that surrounds all of us wants your power."

Power? She didn't have any power, nor did she want any. "There is no darkness," Lyssa argued. "The Isen Demon was defeated, and the children he left behind are just that. *Children.*" She ignored the rumors of powerful magic wielded by demon daughters, and concentrated on the more pleasant stories of perfectly ordinary little girls. She could pick and choose what she wished to believe until her own eyes proved her wrong.

Oh, she did wish the old woman wouldn't smile! A smile on Vellance's face was a terrifying sight.

"Do you think the Isen Demon is the only darkness that blights Columbyana and the lands beyond? There is more darkness than light in this world, girl. The light must fight to remain the stronger of the two." She waved a dismissive hand. "Heed my warning, or don't." The disturbing smile disappeared. "Your life, your path, is your own. Choose well, or you will pay dearly for your foolishness."

It was too much. Lyssa spun around and ran toward her father, her heart pounding, her mouth dry with fear. Why was the fear so strong? Why did her heart beat so hard? She had no magical gifts of any kind. Not dark, not light. She was just a girl with simple dreams of an ordinary life, and Vellance was just an old woman who took sick delight in scaring people she met on the road.

When she glanced back, fearful that Vellance might be following her with more alarming news to impart, the old witch was gone.

Chapter One

Seven years and eleven months later...

The stone wall was slimy and cold and unpleasant, but still Lyssa kept her hand pressed against it. She cherished the feel of the stone because it was solid. It was real. Complete darkness surrounded her, and complete silence took on a sound of its own—the horrifying sound of nothing and no one.

Her heart pounded, her mouth went dry. "Hello?" she whispered. "Is anyone there?" Someone, anyone. Please, dear God, let me not be alone.

Though she could still feel the cold stone floor beneath her feet, she began to sink rapidly, as if the dark room—walls and floor and all—was dropping out from beneath her. Her stomach flipped, she could not find purchase anywhere, and then the floor and the cold wall were gone, and she fell into a pit of nothingness that had no end. She fell and fell, and she screamed...

Lyssa's head popped off the pillow. She was breathing too hard, and beads of perspiration covered her face. Her nightgown was damp with sweat and her palms were sticky. She clutched the sheet beneath her, hanging on for dear life as if she were still falling. The door to her small bedchamber opened, and her stepmother, the still-pretty Sinmora Tempest, stuck her head inside.

"Another bad dream, dear?" Though her voice was light, concern was clear in Sinmora's eyes.

"Yes," Lyssa answered.

"What was it about this time? Do you remember?"

Lyssa sat up and swung her legs over the side of the bed. She rotated her ankles, turned her head and lifted her shoulders, one and then the other.

"No. I don't recall." She hated to lie to her stepmother, but to tell everything would end in frustration for them both. Sinmora Tempest was a woman with her feet planted firmly on the ground. Lyssa had learned long ago that Sinmora had no real patience for concerns about bad dreams or a witch's prophecy. Burned bread. A ripped hem. Too much rain, or not enough. To her stepmother those worries were solid and real, while nightmares were just dreams. A witch's prophecies were allowed even less weight, even when it could be argued that they had, so far, been true. "I'll be in to help you in just a few minutes."

The early morning sun shone softly, breaking through the curtains that hung over an eastern-facing window, washing the small room with a yellowish, warm light. It was not dark here. A dream was just a dream…

She forced her thoughts forward. There was much to do in the next few hours, and she began to check off the chores ahead of her. Such a mental list would often drive the memory of the nightmare that plagued her so deep she could barely remember the details.

Sinmora smiled. "There is no need for you to work in the kitchen with me today. After all, it's your wedding day."

Lyssa refrained from adding "*Again*" in a voice that would surely betray her disappointment.

Sinmora did not mention the old prophecy; she ignored that worry, as always. "You can help your father today, if you'd like. He'll be making a delivery to the palace this afternoon."

Lyssa leaped off the bed and headed for her wardrobe, trying her best to leave the nightmare behind. She didn't have to work on her wedding day, but she liked the palace. It was sprawling and magnificent, and filled with laughter and the high voices of children. She'd heard tales of a time when the palace had been a frightening place, a pile of stones infused with dark magic, a place where people often simply disappeared. But no more. The emperor and empress and their children had turned the palace into a sunny, loving place.

Perhaps a trip there would wipe the nightmare—and the memories—from her mind.

She couldn't help but remember the words Vellance had spoken to her almost eight years earlier. At that time Lyssa had been certain she would be a wife long before the age of twenty-three. But on her first wedding day, not much more than two years after that meeting, Atman Rybar had run off with another woman; his father's insanely beautiful housemaid. Lyssa's heart had been broken, for she had convinced herself that she loved the handsome Atman, and her feelings had been horribly hurt. It was embarrassing to be left for another woman. And a housemaid, at that! Her pride had been wounded; her young heart had been broken.

At the very least, Atman should have made his decision *before* she had made her way to the chapel in her best dress. Being left at the altar had been humiliating; afterward she hadn't left the house for weeks.

Of course, she'd been young, and her heart had mended soon enough. Within a year she'd set another wedding date, this time with the duller and less handsome yet infinitely more stable Tanni Onund, a suitable and unexciting fellow who had managed to get himself trampled by a runaway horse on his way to the chapel.

The third potential groom, the barely adequate Neron Lew, had caught a fever a few days before their wedding date and had died while dragging himself to the chapel, where Lyssa had been waiting anxiously even though marriage would change her name to the entirely unacceptable Lyssa Lew. After losing three grooms, in one manner or another, even her sunny nature couldn't stand the steady barrage of calamity. The nightmares had started. She'd tried to remain optimistic, but she too often felt anxious. Desperate.

After Neron's death, she had not been particularly sought after. In truth, she had not been sought after *at all*. Even those she had initially dismissed as unsuitable prospective husbands avoided her. She knew there were those who called her Bad Luck Lyssa, or Terrible Tempest. Some men actually looked the other way in fear when she caught their eye, as if her very glance might strike them dead.

And all the while she remembered that dreadful witch's words. She refused to give much credence to the talk of magic and darkness and light, because if she did she might lose all hope. If she possessed magic, if there was an unnatural power within her, wouldn't she be aware of it? The one word that she could never shake from her too-vivid memory of that day was *alone*.

She would have liked to think that the man she was to marry today was braver than most, but the truth of the matter was, he was simply as desperate to marry as she was. Kyran Verrel was handsome enough, not particularly smart nor particularly dull. He was average, ordinary. Just what she wanted from life. He came from a poor family who worked a farm not far from Arthes, and he wished for the easier life of a merchant. Marrying a merchant's only child must have seemed like a dream come true to him, even though there were times when Lyssa was almost certain he didn't like her very much. He would learn to like her. She was almost certain he didn't *dislike* her, but now and then she noted an awkwardness between them, an uneasy feeling she could not identify.

But never mind that. She could be very pleasant, when pleasantness was required. She would be a good wife, and Kyran would be glad to claim her as his bride. And she would be married before her twenty-third birthday.

Barely.

They weren't going to bother with the chapel this time around. The priest who'd attempted to preside over her previous three weddings, the thin and often sour Father Kiril, was coming to the house this afternoon. In front of a very small gathering of family and perhaps a friend or two, Lyssa would become a wife. And just in time.

Tomorrow was her twenty-third birthday.

After nearly four years, Blade was finally so close he could smell and taste the culmination of the need for revenge that had driven him to this place. He looked up, taking in the tall palace with its stone walls, solid defenses of impenetrable rock, and its armed sentinels. Somewhere inside that palace was the man who had killed Runa.

Standing on the street, he tried to blend in, to remain unnoticed. His only weapon, a dagger seated in a sheath at his side, was covered by a well worn dark cloak. His boots were dusty, his black beard and hair needed trimming. To anyone who bothered to look, he probably appeared to be a traveler, a new visitor to Arthes who was in awe of the palace before him.

Miron Volker—once a rancher, once a thief, once a soldier, once a murderer—had somehow gotten himself named Minister of Foreign Affairs. Volker was almost as protected as the emperor himself, though he deserved no man's protection. He deserved a dagger through the heart, strong hands choking the last breath out of him or the pain of a poison that would rip apart his insides. The method of death wasn't important. All that mattered was that Volker take his last breath. Soon.

Some might say that Blade should take his complaint to Emperor Jahn, who was, by all accounts, a fair ruler who surely knew nothing of Volker's true past and murderous nature. But Blade didn't trust others to do what had to be done. He didn't trust anyone, not anymore. The emperor was *too* fair, perhaps, and Blade had no proof of his allegations to present. All others who knew for a fact that Volker had killed the young Runa Renshaw were already dead. Blade knew this to be true, because he'd been the one to kill them.

Murderers. Thieves. Unworthy, greedy men. They should all rot in a hellish afterlife, eternally burning, suffering as Runa had suffered. She had been so afraid…

No, the emperor would not take the word of the thief and murderer that Blade had become over that of his own minister. Taking his claim to the authorities, hoping for someone else to deliver justice, was a chance Blade could not, *would not*, take.

Blade realized—had accepted long ago—that in his pursuit of vengeance he had become too much like the men he'd hunted down. He had blood on his hands, and he was not yet done. The end was near, though. So very near.

He had to pull his mind from the pains of the past and what he could not do, and concentrate on the task before him. Getting into the palace wouldn't be easy, but it could be done. He watched people coming and going. He paid attention to who was granted admittance and when.

A pretty girl and an older man exited the palace, eliciting no attention from the guards at the entrance. Father and daughter, he would guess, though it was not impossible that they were wed. Many an older man took a younger woman to wife, especially if he had money, as this man obviously did. His clothing was not official, and while his suit of clothes was fine, it was not that of a wealthy man. Same for the girl with the brown hair and womanly shape, who wore a dress the color of mud. The man was a successful tradesman, perhaps, making a delivery, perhaps taking an order as well. Blade had watched the pair enter a short while earlier, their arms laden with packages wrapped in linen and tied with string. The man and his daughter—or wife—had no trouble getting into, or out of, the palace.

A purpose. Blade needed a purpose—one other than justice—to get him past the guards and through those doors. He had waited long enough. To be so close and not be able to finish the job to which he'd devoted the last four years…

The pretty woman and her old man companion headed his way. She was chattering nervously, urging the man to increase his step. "Come along, Papa," she said in a bright voice. "I don't want to be late for my own wedding." She sounded more anxious than happy, more worried than giddy.

Blade didn't move as they came near, even though the woman was so distracted that she wasn't paying proper attention to those around her. Perhaps she thought if she barreled along without a care in the world anyone who was in her way would clear a path. Blade did not move. He stared at the woman, noting the swell of her breasts and the sway of her hips. The dull color of her clothing made her cheeks seem more pink and her eyes more green.

Did she…shimmer? Just a bit? He blinked hard. No, the momentary glow was an illusion, a trick of the afternoon sunlight.

A moment before she was about to run him down, she veered smoothly, instinctively altering her path. Her skirt brushed against his leg. She was so close her sweet scent filled his nose, his head, and more. The flesh of her face and throat was pale and perfect, and would surely be soft to the touch. The soon-to-be bride glanced up, and their eyes met for a brief moment. Hers were wide and, surprisingly, touched with fear. Why would a bride be fearful? Perhaps her groom was not to her liking. Perhaps she feared the night and the initiation to come.

He knew he should look away to spare the girl the embarrassment of meeting a stranger's gaze, but he did not. Instead he stared into her eyes for the span of a heartbeat. She was a pretty girl with normal worries who had no idea that there were monsters like Volker so near. She was the one who turned away, increasing her pace once more to make her escape and barrel toward wedded bliss.

When the girl and her scent were gone, Blade once more turned his full attention to the palace. Volker was in there, alive and ignorant that his past had followed him to Arthes. He dismissed the bride-to-be from his mind. She lived in another world, a sheltered world so unlike his own that he could not imagine how her mind might work. His own world was not at all simple, and if all went well it was about to end.

Miron Volker quickly ascended the palace steps. Nearing fifty, the Minister of Foreign Affairs was no longer a young man, but his health was good, and he remained active and fit. He needed to be the picture of health and strength if he were to command respect—and fear—once he took the throne.

For some years now, official palace activities had been restricted to the lower floors of the palace. No one had been able to restore the mechanical lifts that had been in use during Emperor Sebestyen's reign; no one had even tried in many years. When *he* ruled, he would put his best scientists and magicians to work on the issue. He rather liked the idea of living on and ruling from Level One, at the top of the palace. At the top of the world.

But one battle at a time. First he needed to unseat Emperor Jahn, and the weapons he needed to make that happen were stored on Level Two.

For all intents and purposes, Level Two was deserted. Or had been, until Volker had taken it over and put it to use. Down the hallway, at the far end where cobwebs and dust gathered, his right hand man waited.

Stasio was unnaturally still. His black robes did not flow when he moved; they were like stone. His hood fell forward, hiding his face. Even from a short distance away, it appeared there was only a vacuum where his face should have been. The wizard was unnatural, disturbing even to Volker. But he was also possessed of great magic, and he was as intent on seeing Jahn ousted as Volker himself was.

"You're certain?" Volker asked as he drew close enough to see the shadow of a chin beyond the hood.

"Fairly certain." Stasio's voice was smooth as silk, without excitement or happiness or a hint of emotion of any kind. "The test will tell."

Stasio walked past Volker, his robes still, his head down. He withdrew a key from his pocket and unlocked the door to a room that had once, long ago, been a fine bedchamber for an empress or a concubine. A woman—

no, a girl—sat upon the bed there. She did not appear to be afraid, or even curious about her new circumstances.

She lifted her head and looked directly at Volker. "Hello," she said, and her voice…her voice was like honey; it called to him, drew him forward. She had the look of a Ksana demon, fair and blue-eyed and uncommonly beautiful. It had been years since he'd captured a new one; he'd begun to think his collection was done.

"Wait here," Stasio said. "I would suggest you not move any closer."

Stasio glided down the hall, but Volker didn't watch to see where he went or what he did. The girl on the bed—the deadliest of demons, if Stasio was correct—held his full attention.

That was a part of her power, or so he had been told.

"Come closer," she said, cocking her head to one side.

"I cannot," Volker said.

The girl pouted, then lifted one hand to brush her golden hair back. She seemed not to even be aware of the manacle on her wrist, even though the chains rattled and the manacle itself had to be heavy and painful. A bloody, raw strip of skin marred her delicate wrist.

"Have you come to feed me?" she asked. "I'm very hungry."

"I will have food delivered to you shortly," he said, fighting the urge to free her, rescue her, be her hero…touch her. If she was what Stasio believed her to be, he would do well to remember the instruction to keep his distance. He hadn't been so cautious all these years only to fall victim to the charms of a child like this one.

Volker didn't respect or crave anything the way he respected and craved power. Even from this distance, he saw and felt the power in the girl before him. There was power in great beauty, yes, but she possessed so much more. And *he* possessed *her*.

Stasio returned with a young man in tow. The boy was likely no older than the beauty on the bed. Sixteen, perhaps. Not a man yet not a child. Volker didn't know what Stasio had promised the boy in return for his assistance, but judging by the ragged condition of his clothing, it was probably nothing more than a loaf of bread.

The girl on the bed turned her attention to the newcomer, and her smile grew wide. "Hello," she said, her voice and her face deceptively sweet.

The boy moved toward the bed. He glanced back at Stasio, who waved him forward with an impatient flick of one pale hand. "She needs a companion," Stasio said sharply. "Someone to talk to. Someone to entertain her."

The boy neared the bed and said, in a wavering voice, "I am pleased to make your acquaintance, Princess."

"Princess?" she responded.

"Lord Stasio...he said your presence here is a secret for now, that the Emperor is protecting you. I thought you'd have an accent, coming from so far away, but from what little I have heard...you sound just like anyone else from Columbyana."

"Will you sit with me?" the demon-child asked, patting the bed. Her chains were covered by the long, flowing sleeves of her gown. Not that the boy had eyes for anything other than her face.

The boy sat. Volker held his breath as Princess—the designation suited her, given her regal power—lifted her hand to touch his cheek. He was fascinated by her and still did not seem to notice the bonds.

"What I most want is a kiss," Princess said. "Would you oblige me?"

The boy literally lost his words as he mumbled what sounded like a positive response and leaned forward. Princess leaned forward, too. Slowly. Deliberately. And in the moment right before her lips met those of the anxious boy, her skin seemed to glow, shimmering green and gold.

For a second or two, the kiss looked like any normal meeting of mouths between two innocent and curious young people who had forgotten that they had an audience. But then the boy bucked, every muscle in his body convulsing in protest. He tried to pull away, but could not. His body stiffened and jerked, and he clutched at the bedcover with desperate fists.

Princess continued on as if they were sharing an increasingly passionate and loving kiss. Eyes closed, gold and green shimmer at a level so low it was almost imperceptible, she moved her mouth over the boy's with relish. Her tongue flicked into and out of his mouth, and as his skin turned gray she sighed in great contentment.

By the time she was done with him, the boy was nothing more than a husk of what he'd once been. Skin gray and wrinkled, face that of an ancient man who had been frightened to death, eyes sunken and sightless, he collapsed onto Princess's lap, dead.

Well, Volker certainly hoped the boy was dead.

Princess licked her lips. "Thank you. I feel much better, now that I have been fed."

Before him sat a Ksana, a half-demon, half-human woman child. The most deadly, the rarest, of the demon daughters.

And he now had three of them in his collection.

Since she was sated and he knew to stay out of her reach, Volker stepped into the room. "I don't know what you were called before you came here, but from here on out you shall be called Princess." She was indeed a Princess, or soon would be.

"As you wish," she said pleasantly. She lifted a hand to brush back a long strand of hair, and he noticed that the bloody scrapes on her wrist had healed completely.

"You will like being mine," he promised. "I will take care of you, and I will love you the way a father should love a daughter." That was what they all craved, according to Stasio. Their human halves craved a father; they longed for love. "You may call me Father, if you'd like."

"Yes, Father." She smiled, ignoring the corpse in her lap. "When will I meet my sisters?"

He was silent for a moment. Princess had a touch of precognition or else she was reading his mind. Either—or both—was possible. The powers of the demons, even the Ksanas, varied. It didn't matter. He would find a way to use all her gifts to his advantage.

"This very afternoon, my dear Princess."

Chapter Two

Lyssa sighed in relief when her groom arrived, a little late but in one piece, and not appearing to be ill or injured. Kyran was well-dressed, his long dark blond hair was nicely styled, but he looked…not at all happy. She wondered what had delayed him. She'd been so worried that assisting her father with the delivery to Empress Morgana would make her late, but still she'd had to wait for Kyran. Did he not realize how anxious she would become when he didn't arrive on time? He knew of her sad past where weddings were concerned, so he should realize how his tardiness would worry her. It was a terrible way to start their new life together.

The room was dismally and sparsely occupied. Her father and stepmother, the holy man who would perform the ceremony, an anxious bride, and a nervous groom who'd arrived alone, without a single family member or friend as his guest. Lyssa was suddenly aware that there was not one cheerful face in the room. Sinmora attempted a smile, but it wasn't genuine and didn't last long. Should both bride and groom be miserable on their wedding day? It didn't seem right, but neither did a lifetime alone. So what was she to do? If the witch's prophecy had been correct, if her dreams of an achingly lonely darkness were more than simple nightmares, then Kyran was her last chance for all that she desired. A family. A home of her own. He was her *last chance* to become a wife before she turned twenty-three. Maybe they would learn to love one another, in time. At the very least, she hoped they would become friends.

She was a little surprised that not one member of Kyran's family had come with him. Was this not a happy occasion, for him to take a wife? Maybe they were angry because he intended to leave the farm. It had already been decided that he would live here and would immediately go to work for her father. Maybe his family knew of her unfortunate past and they were worried for him. Maybe they liked her even less than Kyran did.

Truly, there was nothing she could say about the groom's lack of a wedding party, since none of her own friends had come to the house for this ceremony. They all had very good reasons why they couldn't make it; they were busy with their own husbands and children and responsibilities. But she did wonder if perhaps they simply could not bear the drama of yet another disastrous almost-wedding.

Lyssa lifted her chin, dismissing all her worries as best she could and concentrating on the positive. She *would* be married before she turned twenty-three. Barely, as the sun was about to set on the last day of her twenty-second year, but it was as good as done. Kyran was here, having avoided death and disease on the way to their simple altar, and she was determined to see this done, in spite of her reservations.

Kyran walked over to her and took both her hands in his own. The way he looked into her eyes, the sorrow there...

Oh, no.

"I'm so sorry, Lyssa. I can't do this."

The floor beneath her feet started to spin, much as it had in the morning's nightmare. Her vision narrowed until all she could see was his traitorous, ordinary, not-very-bright face.

"Of course you can," she said, her heart pounding. She could feel it slamming against her chest so hard that surely everyone in the room heard her heartbeat. Her father took a step toward her. The priest sighed and dropped his gaze to the floor. Lyssa stopped her father's approach with a glance and a shake of her head and then she gave Kyran her attention. "If it makes you feel any better, I don't love you, either. There's more than love to marriage. We can make it work. We'll be friends, *partners*. We don't need love."

"I'm in love with someone else," Kyran whispered. "I thought I could do this. I was ready to marry you even though I knew it wasn't right for either of us. I thought it would be enough, to have you beside me as a friend and wife while I worked in your father's shop. Many people live worse lives. But then I met her, and I realized what true love could be."

Patience fading quickly, she snatched her hands from his. "You're leaving me for another woman?"

"Yes." Kyran smiled weakly. "I met her quite by accident, on the road through the woods just last week. Oh, Lyssa, she's so beautiful, so kind, and...I loved her at first glance, and she loves me."

She took a step back, the truth making her feel faint. "I truly do not need to hear this."

Kyran nodded, as if he understood. "We're leaving Arthes immediately. She has family in the Northern Province. Trust me, it's better this way. It would have ended badly for us. You deserve to find a love of your own, to feel what I now feel. Forgive me." With that he bowed curtly and exited the house as if a wolf were on his tail.

Lyssa stared at the door for a long while. Well, it seemed like a long while, as the seconds dragged on. Her parents and Father Kiril remained silent and still, disapprovingly solemn. She had done nothing wrong. She had given them no reason to be displeased with her, but…

Again she felt as if the floor were dropping out from under her, just as it had in her nightmare. The witch had been right. This was the end of her life. She would never marry, never give birth to a child, never have a home of her own. No man would ever love her. She would have no partner in life.

She wished with all her heart that she could convince herself the witch had been wrong all those years ago, but after four failed attempts at becoming a wife, what was she to think? The constant dreams of being alone in a dark room, where no one could see or hear or touch her…they were not only nightmares that woke her with a scream, they were horrifying predictions of her bleak future.

If there truly was a battle between darkness and light going on all around her, the darkness had won. Somehow it was her fault. There must be a weakness in her, something bad that she could not control…

It was Sinmora who broke the silence. "Oh, honey, I'm so sorry." Her hug was warm and genuine, and Lyssa allowed herself to wallow in it for a long moment. "There will be other men. Kyran was likely correct when he said a marriage between you two would go badly. It's a flighty man who meets a woman on the road and instantly thinks himself in love." She pursed her lips in disapproval. "You deserve better, dear. You will find happiness…one day."

Lyssa stepped away from the offered comfort. She steeled her spine, and forced her voice to remain steady and certain. "No, Vellance was right. This was my last chance. I'm going to live at home for the rest of my days." That might be unavoidable, but she didn't have to give in to whatever darkness might attempt to claim her. Besides, the magical part of the prediction could be completely wrong, an attempt by the witch to frighten her. As she had done all those years ago, Lyssa tried to convince herself that she could pick and choose which predictions she would accept and which ones she could dismiss as impossible. Her life would be what she made it, not a pre-ordained nightmare.

She desperately wanted to believe that to be true, even though she was no longer a child who was capable of convincing herself that she could pick apart a prediction and take from it only the tidbits that pleased her.

"I'll work with Papa," she said, swallowing her fear. "I'm good with numbers, and I'm good with people, too. Maybe it's too late for me, maybe I won't have a family of my own, but that doesn't mean I can't make a good life for myself." Her voice almost broke on that last sentence, but she wanted to believe it was true. Who needed a husband? And children were often disappointments to their mothers. Besides, it wasn't as if she looked forward to childbirth. Who would?

"Oh, that ridiculous prediction," Sinmora snapped. "That was nothing more than a crazy old woman's ramblings, and I can't believe you've taken it seriously all these years. You *will* marry. You *will* have a family." She reached out to caress Lyssa's hair. "You *will* know love."

Lyssa wished she could believe that.

The priest left the house without ever looking the "bride" in the eye. Lyssa refused Sinmora's offers of a bite of supper, gave her father—who'd been silent and obviously disappointed through it all—a hug, and went to bed early. The narrow bed where she'd slept as a child would be her bed for life now, unless she decided to take vows at a nunnery. She shuddered at the thought. Not that the Sisters of Orianan weren't fine women who had dedicated their lives to doing good, but it was not Lyssa's dream to cut her hair and dress forever in black, and go months at a time without speaking a word aloud. Vow of silence? Horrors. Sacrifice was not in her nature. Neither was silence.

No, her father needed her. She was his only child, and she would do her duty and assist him in his trade. As there was no son to whom he could leave his assets, no son by marriage to assist him in his business, she would become like a son to him. Perhaps that was unconventional, but if it was that or a nunnery, her choice was an easy one.

There were worse ways to live her life, she supposed.

Eventually she fell into a deep sleep in the small bed she'd expected to share with a husband on this night, where the dreams of loneliness and darkness were more severe than ever before. The room where she found herself was so dark she couldn't see her own hand in front of her face, and when she began to fall, as she always did, she did not scream. Instead she accepted. She accepted the loneliness, the darkness…the disappointment. Why had she fought it all these years? Fear tried to rise within her, but she pushed it down; she fought it off and focused on the truth. This was her life now.

Briefly, something glimmered silver in the darkness. A knife. No, a sword, long and sharp and deadly. It teased her, made her believe that she was not alone after all. She should have been afraid of the blade, but…it would never hurt her. She knew that as one could know things in a dream. And then it was gone. Lyssa spread her arms and held her breath as she fell, and woke to the silent darkness of her lonely bed chamber, her body lurching a bit as if she actually had fallen from above.

As usual, she tried to see the bright side of the situation. This might all be for the best. She would probably hate having a husband who would no doubt want to tell her what to do every hour of the day, as some husbands did. She wasn't all that sure about sharing a bed with a man, anyway. From all she'd heard, which wasn't much, marital relations were messy and bothersome and perhaps only *occasionally* pleasurable. The act was for creating life and for a man's release. At least, that is what she'd taken from what she'd heard. To hear her married friends tell it, their husbands were quite disagreeable if they did not get their way in the bedroom. Not that they shared everything with her. Because she was an unmarried woman, they deemed some conversations unfit for her virginal ears.

For as long as Lyssa could remember, her father had been overly protective of his only child, shielding her from those he deemed unsavory or unsuitable and protecting her from the harshness of life. Sinmora had not prepared her stepdaughter for marriage, instead saying that it was a husband's place to instruct his bride as he saw fit. This statement was always followed by a flush of her cheeks and a quick turn away.

Lyssa didn't care. Not anymore. There would be no husband to instruct her. No conversations of intimate matters with married friends. Her life had taken a different turn. Lying in the dark she had to wonder…Had her prospective grooms met misfortune or loved another because she'd chosen them? Or had she chosen them because, in the deepest, darkest part of herself, she had somehow known what was to come? She didn't want to think that two men had died simply because she'd agreed to marry them. She preferred to think that she'd chosen them because they were meant to die. There was less weight on her conscience that way. If she possessed any magical abilities at all, that was the extent of it. What a worthless bit of magic *that* was!

She tried to convince herself that she would be fine, but silent tears fell from her eyes and slipped down her cheeks. While self-pity was not an attractive trait in anyone, she decided she deserved to feel sorry for herself, at least for one night. She would be strong tomorrow.

As she cried, her stomach growled. She shouldn't have skipped supper. Maybe there were a lot of "shouldn'ts" in her life, but at the moment that was the big one. She was hungry. This problem she could fix. Lyssa threw back the coverlet and left her bed, heading for the main room where earlier in the day she'd almost become a bride. The large room was used as a sitting area for family and for visitors, and in one corner there sat a stove and work space where meals were prepared. There was also a small table there, just right for three. As she headed for that table she thanked her lucky stars that this house also had two small but private bed chambers; one for her and one for her father and Sinmora. As she would apparently be living here for a very long time, having her own room—however small—was a luxury.

She and Kyran had decided to live here for a while after the wedding that hadn't been, but the plan had been to soon have a place of their own. Their own small house, their own kitchen. A home they could share, just the two of them, until babies started to arrive. And now…now she couldn't even imagine having her own home. It was such a simple desire. She did not wish for wealth or great beauty or power. Just a couple of rooms she could call her own.

Her father and stepmother were still awake, talking. She heard their muffled voices from beyond their closed bed chamber door as she uncovered a half loaf of bread. She tried to be quiet as she cut a slice. There was no need to disturb them, and if they knew she was up and about they would probably feel obligated to attempt to soothe her. She did not wish to be soothed. She wished to wallow in misery for a while longer.

Their voices were low but carried well; *too* well as those voices rose slightly. She didn't try to listen, that would be rude, but a word caught her attention, and the knife she'd been wielding stopped moving mid-slice.

Baby.

Lyssa didn't move for a moment as her hand clenched on the handle of the knife. Her bare toes curled on the smooth wooden floor. Perhaps one of their friends was going to have a child, she reasoned. Sinmora was a few years younger than her husband and she had several younger acquaintances who had many children. Though it wasn't a subject they discussed openly with their daughter, Lyssa knew they had always wanted babies. It simply hadn't happened. Sinmora was nearly forty years old, far too old to have another child. *Far* too old.

More words drifted her way.

"Maybe it's a boy. You always wanted a son."

"You must be careful. I'm worried."

"When will we tell Lyssa?"

"Let's wait. She's had a difficult day, and this news will come as quite a shock."

Lyssa didn't breathe for a long moment.

"Cyrus, we must find her a proper husband."

Lyssa's knees went weak. She could no longer fool herself into thinking that they were talking about someone else. This house was about to become a bit crowded. Would she be sharing a room with the new baby, or would the child stay in the room where her parents slept? If the baby was a boy, her father would finally have a son to carry on his trade. She'd never realized that her father wanted a son so badly, that she was undoubtedly a disappointment simply because she was a girl. She should have known. Men always wanted sons.

Her already horrid day took an abrupt turn for the worse. She would be nothing but a burden, a daughter long past marriageable age who continued to live at home. Another mouth to feed, an old maid, an embarrassment to the family. No man would have her after four failed attempts at becoming a bride, and if the witch had been right, her window for marriage would close in mere hours. A nunnery was beginning to seem like a good idea.

In the near distance, bells rang, counting down the hours of the day. Each peal shot through her, and she held her breath as she silently counted. How many hours until she turned twenty-three? The peals ended and she held her breath. Two hours until midnight. Two hours until she turned twenty-three and all hope was lost.

Her heart leapt; her hands trembled. The witch had said her path was her own, that her future was in her hands. Did that mean there was something she could do about her current predicament? Could she save herself from a life of loneliness instead of feeling sorry for herself and waiting for someone else to save her?

Two hours to find a husband and take her vows. Two hours to become a wife, well and true. Wedded and bedded. Eight years ago she hadn't understood exactly what that meant. She was older now, and she even though she had not been well-instructed when it came to marital relations, she understood well enough.

A fresh thought occurred to her. She was to be married by twenty-three. There was nothing in the witch's prediction that said the husband she took before twenty-three would be her *only* husband. Maybe the *who* didn't matter at all, simply the time and date. Dissolution ceremonies were rare, but not unheard of. If she took a man as husband tonight strictly to fulfill the obligation to be a wife before her twenty-third birthday, maybe it would buy her some time to find the *right* man.

If the right man for her was out there. Somewhere.

Lyssa ran toward her bedchamber to dress. She had two hours to find a man and convince him to marry her. More accurately, two hours to marry and consummate the marriage. Vellance had been clear enough about that. She had to be a real wife before midnight.

All she needed was a willing man. Fortunately for her, any man would do.

Chapter Three

The roar of the tavern surrounded and engulfed Blade, drowned out his thoughts and dulled the pain a little, much as the whisky he'd consumed earlier this evening had done. Wearing a stolen sentinel's uniform, sitting alone in the corner of the tavern, he waited for someone to realize that he was the man who'd tried to walk into the palace hours earlier, even though he was almost certain no one in this tavern would look twice at a solitary sentinel.

The afternoon had not gone as planned. He hadn't bargained on the inquisitive guard at the palace gate, the battery of questions or the young and annoyingly vigilant sentinel who had given chase when Blade's answers to those questions had proven unsatisfactory.

It had not been his finest moment.

Fortunately for him, the other patrons in this less than fine establishment were as drunk as he—most were drunker, in fact—and cared nothing for the emperor's security. Not tonight. Things might look different by the light of day. He would have to ditch the stolen uniform, perhaps shave the beard and cut his hair. But not tonight. Tonight was for drowning his sorrows and frustration in mediocre whisky. He might also ease his frustration in the arms of a woman—it was certainly well past time—but those women who worked here laughed too harshly, painted their faces garishly, and were not at all indiscriminate about who shared their beds. They were too scantily dressed, and too sweetly perfumed in an attempt to hide the fact that they did not care for bathing regularly. While he did on occasion miss a woman's touch and give over to his natural urges, not just any woman would do.

Before Runa had died, there had been a woman. Four years ago, with the age of twenty-five fast approaching, he had considered asking a pretty girl to marry him, making a home in the village by the sea where he had been born. He'd thought himself in love with her, though now he wondered if what he'd felt had been love or simpler lust. Whatever it was, love or lust, he'd been willing to give up his vocation as a privateer in order to take a wife. He'd apprenticed with a shipbuilder as a lad, and with those skills and his savings he could have started a small business of his own.

Such simple plans for a normal life, but he'd never actually asked that pretty girl to marry him. Tonight—for the past couple of years, he admitted—he could barely remember her face. He realized, half drunk, that whatever it had been that he'd felt for that girl had died a natural death a long time ago, along with his plans for a simple life. In his heart everything had been replaced by his need for vengeance.

He'd forgotten the details of the pretty girl's appearance, but he remembered Runa's face in great detail. He remembered it too well. That moment when his little sister had seen him and no doubt wondered where he'd been, as she'd surely wondered why he hadn't come to save her...He remembered. He'd been running, shouting, but he was too far away. She'd been surrounded by five men in sentinel uniforms and one who wore a long black cloak. Her hands had been bound in front of her as if she were a criminal. He remembered that second when their eyes met, right before Miron Volker's sword pierced her body. He had not known Volker's name then, he had just been the man in the black cloak. Runa had screamed Blade's name. Only once. He had been looking his little sister in the eye when that sword plunged into her heart and sent her to the ground, boneless. Dead.

She'd been eleven years old.

Runa would likely not recognize him if she saw him now. She would turn away in fear from the man he had become. Physically, beneath the beard and the long hair, he was much the same as he had been, but inside he was too much like the men who had kidnapped and killed her. Men who would do anything to achieve their goals. Men who had no conscience, no honor. No heart.

He unconsciously fingered the scar beneath his tunic, the scar near his heart that reminded him of the near-killing wound Volker had delivered as Blade had rushed to his sister's body.

The door to the tavern opened, and several heads turned to see who was joining the celebration. Blade felt a jolt of mild surprise when he recognized the woman he'd seen exiting the palace just that afternoon; the silly nit who had almost run him over on the way to her wedding. Had she lost her groom so soon? That did not bode well for the marriage. She closed the door behind her and glanced around the room, occasionally rising up on tiptoes and craning her neck. Yes, it looked as if she was searching for someone. She bit her lower lip and wrung her hands; it was painfully obvious that she did not belong here.

Not that any lost girl was his problem.

She took a deep breath and walked more deeply into the room. The tables were so close together that she sometimes had to turn sideways to carefully squeeze between the backs of two chairs. Her eyes landed on one young, clean-shaven boy, and she stopped, leaning down to speak to him. Her face was deadly serious, and yet the boy laughed. If that was her husband, she was in for a long and tiresome marriage. But she moved on to another table and another man. Blade took a long swig of whisky, then poured another glass from the bottle sitting on his table. The clink of glass on glass was loud, yet also soothing, somehow. Again there was harsh laughter, but this time, the gnarly red-haired man the woman attempted to pass didn't allow her to move on.

Gnarly Red grabbed her hand; she yanked it away. He snatched at the fabric of her brown dress, and this time escape was not so easy for her. She slapped his hand, and all those at the table of rowdy farmers and tradesmen laughed. One of Red's companions reached up and grabbed sloppily at the swell of her breast. She was openly offended, shocked by the outrageous behavior.

Blade sipped at his whisky. Well, what did she expect, coming into a place like this one all alone? Served her right. And where was her husband? What a wastrel he was, to allow his woman to wander the night. If *he* had been the pretty girl's new husband and this was their wedding night, neither of them would be wasting a moment in this place. They would be in bed, sweating and sore and spent. A woman like this one put the painted ladies in the room to shame. Not that she would give the man he'd become the time of day.

In a haughty voice touched with a fear she could not disguise, she demanded that Red release her, a demand that was once again met with raucous laughter, as well as an indelicate suggestion. There was stark terror on her face now, terror so fresh and real that Blade turned away from it. This was not his fight. He had a mission of his own, a purpose, and it wasn't in his nature to go about rescuing damsels in distress. Especially if she happened to be a foolish damsel who should have known to remain in the safety of her own home after dark.

Out of the corner of his eye, he saw the girl being pulled awkwardly onto Red's lap. She immediately tried—unsuccessfully—to stand and step away. Though she tried again and again to escape, the fellow who hung onto her was too strong.

"I'm simply looking for a proper husband," she said, and though she tried to sound calm, there was fear in her voice. "*You* will not do."

By now everyone in the tavern was watching the scene unfold.

"If you need a husband. I'll be glad to fill the position!" one old man shouted.

"You've already got a wife," his friend said loudly. "And you haven't filled *anything* in years!"

More laughter, louder this time.

"I'll marry you!" a drunken man in the back of the tavern yelled. His words slurred. "Come sit on my lap, lovey, and we'll talk about it."

More men joined in.

"I'll be your husband, but first I'll need to make sure you'll be a proper wife, if you know what I mean."

"I have no coin, but my cock is mighty, or so I have been told."

Blade was compelled to look at the woman's face once more. She no longer attempted to appear collected. She was terrified, and growing more so with every ribald suggestion.

"This was a mistake," she said, raising her shaking voice to be heard above the roar. "Just…just let me go and I'll leave."

Blade sighed. The way some of these wastrels were looking at her, if she left the tavern on her own she wouldn't get far.

"What if I don't want to let you go?" the red-haired man who had captured her said, loudly enough for the entire assemblage to hear.

"Please." Her voice was too soft for Blade to hear, though he could read her lips well enough.

Red pinched her, and she squealed. He grabbed her breast with a dirty hand, and she screamed, now fighting even more ardently to escape. And then her captor began to slowly pull up her skirt.

"Someone help me," the lost bride cried as she fought back ineffectually with soft white hands. "Please, help!"

Blade pushed his chair back and slowly stood. "Well, fuck."

Her heart thundered and her vision blurred and grew gray at the edges. She'd been a fool to come here. All she wanted was to escape, to breathe fresh air and run home and hide in her bed. Nightmares were better than this.

God help me! She would happily join a nunnery, Lyssa thought as she slapped away the hands that groped at her, even if she did have to take a vow of silence. She would much prefer to be alone and forever silent than to pass another moment in this horrible man's company. Was that her destiny? To be forever alone?

Not so long ago a life without companionship had seemed the worst possible outcome, but as she desperately struggled in an attempt to escape, she knew there was something much worse than loneliness. Joining a nunnery would free her father from the burden of her care for a lifetime, and it would give her a purpose. It wasn't a purpose which had appealed to her until now, but she'd do anything to escape from this tavern without harm. Besides, there wasn't a suitable husband in the lot! She would gladly cut off all her hair, wear scratchy and unattractive clothing, and pass her every waking hour caring for the less fortunate. It was that or *become* one of the less fortunate.

Yes, there were worse fates than being alone.

"Let her go."

Lyssa's head snapped around. The man standing behind her had approached soundlessly, or else she had been too terrified to hear anything beyond the men's crude suggestions and her own heartbeat. Whatever the reason, she'd had no idea he was there until he spoke.

"Why should I?" the man who held her asked with a grin, once more revealing his lack of dental hygiene in the gaps where teeth should've been.

"Because if you don't, I'm going to kill you," the newly arrived man said calmly.

He wore a sentinel's uniform but carried no sword. His only weapon was a small knife, which remained seated in its sheath at his belt. A big man, he stood more than a head taller than she. *Much* more. His shoulders were broad, his hands large and his legs long. She had not realized sentinels could be so unkempt. She was shocked that the emperor allowed such lack of care among his men. The sentinel's black beard was shaggy and had not been trimmed in quite some time—if ever. His hair, black as night, was tangled and long, and in need of a good washing. It looked as if it had never seen a comb. He looked…wild.

But it was his eyes that held her attention. Given his coloring, they should have been as black as his hair, or at least a deep brown, but instead they were a brilliant blue. A brilliant blue that appeared to be without emotion of any kind. Cold as ice, they were. He threatened to kill the man who restrained her with as much heat as he might ask for a glass of ale, and yet she had no doubt that he would do as he said.

The man he spoke to must have recognized that just as she did. He released her suddenly, and as she leapt to her feet he gave her a shove that sent her reeling into the unkempt sentinel. "Take her, then. There's no need for you to look at me that way. I was just having a bit of fun."

Lyssa fell against the sentinel's chest. He caught her with one arm, righting her quickly and then releasing her. The crude suggestions had stopped. The tavern patrons returned to their private conversations, glancing now and then toward her and her rescuer.

She never should have come to a tavern looking for a husband, but at this hour and with time being of the essence, what other choice did she have?

"Will you see me home?" she asked the bearded man who had saved her. She'd come here on her own, but now she was terrified of stepping into the night without an escort.

"Why should I?" he asked, not even bothering to look at her.

"I'll pay you," she said softly. "Gold coin." She didn't have much in the way of savings, but the sentinel could have it all if he would just get her out of here.

He turned his head then and stared down at her with those arresting eyes. That was when she realized that she'd met him before, outside the palace on this very afternoon. Well, they hadn't *met*, exactly, but she'd almost run him down. He'd stared at her just this way for a split second.

"I don't need coin."

"Please," she whispered. "I'm afraid to go out there by myself."

He grabbed her arm too tightly and guided her toward the exit without even a hint of gentleness. "You were not afraid when you came here on your own," he said, his tone accusing. He was annoyed with her, though nothing that had happened was her fault. Not really. "What were you thinking? That new husband of yours should give you a good thrashing."

"I don't have a new husband," she said sharply as the sentinel pushed through the door and all but dragged her onto the street. How did he know that today was supposed to be her wedding day? The rush of fresh, cool air was a delight after the crush of unwashed bodies in the crowded tavern, and she took a long, deep breath. It didn't matter how he knew; he did. "And if I did have a husband, he would not dare to thrash me."

"I heard you mention a wedding just a few hours ago. What happened?"

Lyssa lifted her chin. There was her explanation, then. He'd overheard her mention the wedding on the street, and had remembered. "What happened is none of your business." As if she wasn't humiliated enough already!

"What were you doing in there?" he asked angrily.

She pursed her lips, reluctant to tell the sentinel that she'd walked into the tavern in search of a husband. Her plan sounded so foolish, now.

He leaned in, too close, "And don't tell me that's none of my business, because I just left a half-full bottle of whisky sitting on a table in order to save your silly ass."

Silly? She was many things, and she was not perfect, but…silly? She took a deep breath but declined to offer an argument. She had bigger problems than what a strange man thought of her.

Hmm. Was he a strange and *unmarried* man? What did she have to lose? She'd reached rock bottom, searching an establishment like this one for a mate—however temporary that mate might be. And unkempt as he was, the sentinel did possess at least a modicum of decency. "I need a husband, and it must be done by midnight or else I will never wed." There was so little time left that she was almost resigned to the nunnery. *Almost.*

She looked up and squinted, trying to see beyond the awful beard to the man beyond, not that it mattered. He was younger than she'd first thought, and beyond the hair and eyes he might be pleasant-looking. At least he had all his teeth, as far as she could tell. He had the other patrons of the tavern beat hands down, as he had been the only one to come to her aid in a time of crisis. If there had been other sentinels present they might have assisted as well, but he had been alone.

Still, he had to possess some admirable qualities beneath all that hair.

"Are you married?" she asked.

There wasn't much light on the street, just the glow from a streetlamp and a bit of a moon, but she was sure she saw a flash of emotion of some sort in his eyes. "No," he responded.

"The life of a sentinel is very precarious, I imagine." They didn't make much in the way of pay, but she thought that fact would be too indelicate to mention. "Have you ever given any thought to marrying?"

"None."

"Oh." She glanced around the deserted street. She hadn't been afraid on her way to the tavern, but now it seemed that danger waited around every corner. A shiver ran down her spine. The night was too much like her nightmares, dark and fathomless and lonely. She pushed that thought away, forcing herself to focus on the urgent matter at hand. "What if it wasn't a real marriage at all, but rather a favor for a new friend?"

"You're not my friend."

Lyssa gathered her courage, what was left of it, and looked the sentinel in the eye. "I need a husband by midnight. Don't ask me to explain why now," she added quickly, "because there's not much time left before tomorrow arrives. It has occurred to me that though I must be a wife by midnight, it needn't be a permanent marriage at all, but could be an arrangement that would satisfy a particular requirement until other, more suitable, arrangements can be made. So, what do you say? Will you marry me? Temporarily, of course."

For a long moment the sentinel was silent. Then he asked, "What would I get out of the bargain?"

"What do you want?" Time was running out. He could name his price.

"If we're man and wife, I might decide I'd like to fuck you."

"All right," she said quickly, and then she bit her lower lip. "What is that, exactly?"

The sentinel sighed. "You're a virgin, aren't you?"

"Of course I am," she responded. "What did you expect? I'm not like one of those women in the tavern, I'm…" And then she realized what he was most likely referring to. "Oh, I think I understand. Yes, that will be required as part of the bargain." It wasn't as if she wasn't curious. She should have become a wife in all ways years ago. Besides, the witch had said she needed to be married and bedded before she turned twenty-three, which didn't give them much time. She wondered if there was time to arrange for the sentinel to have a bath. "We'll take care of that as soon as the vows are spoken. Is there anything else you want from the arrangement?"

Again he was silent for a long moment. The delay made Lyssa rise up on her toes in frustration, and then drop down again.

Finally he spoke. "I saw you and an old man leaving the palace today. Do you go there often?"

"My father is a shopkeeper, and he's not an old man. Perhaps he is well on his way, but he has many years left in him."

"That does not answer my question."

"He makes occasional deliveries to the palace, and sometimes I help."

"That will do, I suppose," he whispered, his voice like velvet, smooth and deep and assured.

Precious moments ticked past. "*What* will do?"

"I will marry you, if you'll promise to get me into the palace."

That made no sense at all. "But you're a sentinel. Surely you have access to the palace." She felt as if something was crawling beneath her skin, she was so anxious to have this done. A temporary marriage to this man, who was a far cut above the others she'd encountered tonight, would solve all her problems. At least, she believed that to be the case. It was certainly worth a try, especially since it was all she had.

"I'm not a sentinel," he said. "I stole this uniform."

"If you're not a sentinel, then what do you do?" And why on earth would he steal a uniform?

"I travel. I do jobs where I find them, when I need them. Once I was a sailor and a shipbuilder, but that was long ago. Now I am no one. I am nothing."

She'd always loved the sea, but his connection to sailing and ships was in the past. Now he was a drifter, a beggar who stole clothes—and yet he managed to have enough coin to buy a bottle of whisky, which meant it was likely he'd stolen more than a uniform.

And he was her last chance.

A thief or a nunnery? A complete stranger or a life lived alone? What did it say about her that the thief seemed a better choice? "We must hurry," she said, tugging on his stolen uniform and leading the way to the church at the center of town. It had already been a while since the newly installed palace clock had pealed, announcing the eleventh hour. She wasn't certain how much time she had left to wake Father Kiril and convince him to perform an untraditional wedding ceremony before that clock struck midnight. "By the way, what's your name?" she asked as she turned into a narrow lane.

"Blade Renshaw," her prospective groom said.

Blade. Unusual name. For a brief moment, Lyssa pictured the sword from her latest dream. The dangerous, sharp, gleaming blade had swung so close...

"My name is Lyssa," she said, pushing the memory of the dream to the back of her mind. "Lyssa Tempest. Soon to be Lyssa Renshaw, I suppose."

Considering her unfortunate history with prospective grooms, she wondered if she could keep Blade Renshaw alive and willing until they reached the priest and the marriage could be done.

Chapter Four

Blade willingly followed Lyssa down wide streets and narrow alleyways, past closed shops and stone houses where residents slept. Even though they passed through many dark shadows untouched by moonlight or the infrequent street lamps, she did not falter. She knew the way, as one who'd lived in Arthes all her life should.

It didn't take long for the cool night air to sober him. The mental fog he'd found in the whisky faded, and he was left clear-headed and impatient. The woman who guided him through the city had not been in his plans even a few minutes ago, and now she was his best chance of achieving his goal.

He shouldn't be curious about Lyssa Tempest and her need for a husband by a certain hour, but he was. A little. For the life of him, he could not figure out why a pretty woman—one of a class that allowed her to walk into and out of the palace—had to go to such lengths to get a husband, or why she felt that the deed had to be done before midnight. He could not deny his curiosity, but in truth her motivations didn't matter.

She could get him into the palace. Perhaps not tomorrow, or even next week, but eventually he would walk through the main entrance, and once he was inside he would find Volker and take his revenge. He would almost certainly make Lyssa a widow in the process, but she would already have gotten what she wanted out of the bargain, too; a husband before the last strike of the clock on this particular day.

Perhaps before he went to die he would ask her what had led her to this point, but the truth of the matter was, it didn't matter. She served his purpose, just as he served hers.

Lyssa rounded the church, and along the side wall she found and knocked on a small door. She had to knock several times before a sleep-rumpled priest answered. He wore a nightshirt and a cap, both thin with wear, and carried a single candle.

"What's wrong?" the priest asked, sounding more alert than he looked. "Is your father ill? Sinmora?" he continued without giving her a chance to respond. "Wait while I dress." He started to turn away, but Lyssa stopped him with her words.

"Marry us, Father Kiril. Right here, and quickly. *Now.*"

The priest stopped, turned slowly, lifted his eyes to look at Blade with curiosity. "Just this afternoon—"

"I know very well what happened this afternoon," Lyssa interrupted sharply.

"I cannot…."

"You can," she insisted.

Father Kiril turned his full attention to the insistent woman. "Lyssa, dear, this is highly unusual and totally unacceptable. I cannot—I *will not*—marry you to a stranger in the middle of the night. We'll meet tomorrow, I'll get to know your…" The priest cleared his throat. Twice. "… most recent betrothed, and—"

"That will not do, I'm afraid. How can I make you understand?" She sighed, once. "Fine, here's the truth," she snapped. "Years ago a witch told me that if I didn't become a wife before I turned twenty-three I would never marry." Her words were clipped and fast. "Actually, she said I would be alone forever. *Forever*, Father Kiril. I don't like to be alone. Who does? I would not believe her. I tried not to believe her. But you know very well what my history in that matter has been like. And I have dreams of the terrible darkness and loneliness that will come to me if I don't marry. *Now*."

"Lyssa, dear…" The priest shook his head.

"If I don't marry I will be a burden to my father always, or else I will be forced to join a nunnery."

"The Sisters of Orianan do good work," the priest argued.

Midnight was coming, and it was clear to Blade that if he and Lyssa weren't wed by then it would not be done at all. If he let her slip away, his best chance at gaining entrance to the palace would be gone.

"Father Kiril," Blade said, calling upon his most dignified voice, the voice of the man he had once been. "Lyssa's reasoning aside, I pledge to be a good husband to her. And in order to thank you for your service in this hour, I also pledge to make a generous donation to the church."

The priest's spine straightened. "Why is it that I do not know you, son?"

Blade looked the priest in the eye, as if he had nothing to hide. Lying to a man of God was not his most egregious sin, not by a long shot. It was not even his most egregious sin committed on this long day. "I have only recently arrived in Arthes. The moment I saw Lyssa, I knew she was the only woman for me. If she has had misfortunes when it comes to marriage, then it is only because the fates were saving her for me." Perhaps fate was not the proper argument, considering who was on the receiving end of this discussion. "God has brought us together. If it makes her happy to say our vows at this late hour and in such an unusual way, I will not deny her. I will be a good husband. I will give her everything she wants of me." No need to reveal that all she wanted from him was a marriage ceremony and a bedding.

Lyssa stared at him, wide-eyed. He had managed to surprise her.

"Well, then," the priest said, "since you swear that you will be a good husband to this child I have known all her life, and as you pledge a much needed donation to this church, how can I refuse?"

They were shown in through the rear door and led down a small hallway to the chapel proper. Father Kiril held his candle high, lighting their path a few steps at a time. The walls were a dark polished wood, plain, without any adornment, but also fine and well constructed. The air was sweet; it smelled of incense and candle wax and the oil that was used to polish the walls and furnishings.

Lyssa was in such a hurry to have the marriage done, she insisted that the priest perform the ceremony in his sleep clothes. The priest sighed in dismay but he quickly consented. He did have to leave them for a moment to wake the maid, so there would be a proper witness. Before Father Kiril left the chapel he lit three fat candles so Lyssa and her midnight groom would not be left in the dark while they waited.

It was a fine chapel, Blade noted, lit by those three candles. The flames danced, stirred by an unseen draft from one door or another. As in the hallway, the walls were constructed of fine dark wood, polished with oil and gleaming. The altar was constructed of a paler wood, but it, too, shone in the candlelight. The benches provided for worshippers were more roughhewn, but hardly the worst he had seen. They looked sturdy, well-built and well worn. When he tried to get Lyssa to sit on one of those benches while they waited for the priest, she refused, unable or unwilling to be still even for a moment.

She fidgeted as they waited, no doubt worried about the rapid approach of her twenty-third birthday.

Blade wanted to tell her that witches were often wrong, that they sometimes lied for their own amusement or simply did not know all they claimed to know. He wanted to tell her that the witch who'd predicted for him a happy life, marriage and sons and daughters, had been far off the mark, and it was more than likely that her frightening prediction was also false.

But if he reasoned with her and won, he would lose this opportunity. He'd sacrificed much to get this close to Volker, and he had no qualms about using a woman he barely knew.

Father Kiril returned with a sleep-rumpled housekeeper. The priest had grabbed a heavy robe along the way, so his appearance was a bit more dignified than it had been when he'd opened the door to Lyssa's unusual request. The ceremony was simple and quick. Blade and his bride exchanged vows, promising eternal commitment; a prayer was said. When it was done and the priest declared them man and wife, Lyssa released a long sigh of relief. And still the bells announcing midnight did not ring.

Father Kiril yawned and bade them good evening, and then Blade and his wife exited the church the way they'd come and once again found themselves alone with the night.

"It's done," Lyssa said as they walked out of the alley and onto the main street, which was all but deserted at this hour. In the distance, a drunkard trying to find his way home stumbled along. "And you are still alive!"

"That surprises you?"

"Well, I have had difficulties with potential husbands in the past. A couple of them died on the way to the church."

"That would have been nice to know beforehand," Blade muttered.

Lyssa laughed nervously. "If I'd told you all of my wedding disaster history, you would have run from me."

"That bad?"

"That bad. But it is done now. I am a wife, and it is not yet midnight."

She looked at him and smiled, and in the glow of the moon and a streetlamp straight ahead, she looked even more beautiful than before. His body tightened; he ached.

"You must fuck me. Now."

He was taken aback at her nonchalant use of the crude word he'd thrown at her before. Taken aback and oddly aroused. Clearly she did not *know* it was a crude word. He hadn't realized there was such innocence left in the world.

Her chin came up stubbornly when she saw him hesitating. "It's nothing to worry about, I suppose. I was rather prepared to endure my wifely duties tonight, before my previous groom left me for a…" She stuttered a bit. "F-for another woman." She looked very much as if she were about to change her mind. "I barely know you, and you are in desperate need of a bath and a shave. And perhaps a kiss would serve as well as a, well, the other."

"It's up to you," Blade said gently, as they walked slowly away from the church. *His* strides were long and slow. Lyssa's were shorter and quicker as she attempted to match his pace. "As the priest said, the Sisters of Orianan do good work. I hear they minister to the sick and care for a number of orphans, and take in the most indigent. Some of them have taken on the task of educating the daughters of the Isen Demon, those who seem to be capable of redemption." His heart hitched, a bit, but he felt no guilt. He would do or say whatever was necessary to make this marriage real. Otherwise, he suspected his way into the palace would disappear like fog burned away by a morning sun. "Only a few nuns have died because they were mistaken about the intentions of a demon child or two. They also pray a lot, I imagine, and—"

"I suppose a kiss to seal the marriage will not do," she interrupted. "Do you have a room?"

"I do."

"Is it nearby?"

The first peal announcing midnight rang, and his bride twitched visibly.

"Not *that* nearby." He took her hand and led her quickly toward the closest alleyway.

As he pulled her into darkness, she asked, on a whispered breath, "Here?"

The second peal echoed.

"It's here or not at all, if you wish the deed done before tomorrow arrives." And suddenly he was anxious to have it done, to have her. Not only because she was a means to an end, not only because she could lead him into the palace and straight to Volker, but because she called to him as a woman. He wanted her, wanted to be inside her, to make her scream.

"Fine," she said again, with a sigh that coincided with the third peal. "What am I supposed to do?"

"Nothing." Blade lifted her skirt and slipped his hand between her thighs. She was startled, jumping a bit as the fourth bell rang out. Her skin was wonderfully soft, her response untaught and arousing. This woman who had never been touched by a man was ripe and hungry in a way she undoubtedly didn't understand. The fifth bell rang, and he found the nub at her entrance. She was surprised by her reaction to the touch; her body responded. Her hips rocked gently and she uttered a soft, "Oh." The sixth bell rang, and he slipped a finger inside her. She was wet, but not wet enough, so he stroked and teased as the seventh and eighth bell rang.

She gasped and moved against him. He fell into her, breathed in her sweet scent.

"Shouldn't you..." she said breathlessly. "This feels strangely nice. I didn't really expect...*oh*...but it's not...There's no time, Blade, not nearly enough time."

The ninth bell rang on the tail end of her words, and he freed his erection. He lifted her up, guided his length to her wet heat, and slowly, as the tenth bell rang, he pushed the head of his cock inside her. She gasped, and her hands clutched at his shoulders. He pushed a little bit deeper. She was tight, wet, hot, inexperienced, and ignorantly awaiting something she didn't understand.

He held her up, so her back rested lightly against the wall behind her, and as the eleventh bell peeled he pushed deeper. She gasped as he thrust, breaking past her maidenhead. One more thrust and he filled her completely. With the final peal of the palace bells, by any law or custom he and Lyssa were man and wife.

Princess—that was her name now, and she rather liked it—woke with a start as the bells marking midnight pealed beyond her window. Their new Father did not call either of the others Princess, as he called her. She was his favorite, perhaps because he saw that she was the most powerful of them all. Princess. She liked the sound of her new name, even though it only resonated in her head and not against the stone walls that surrounded her. She remained imprisoned, but she'd been moved to a new room and was no longer alone. She did not like being alone, as she had been for so much of her lifetime.

She had lived in much worse places than this one in her almost-sixteen years. Even before she'd come into her power, she'd been shunned by those who knew the circumstances of her birth. She'd slept in harder beds, or on the floor or the ground. This was a very nice prison.

There were three other beds in this large chamber. Two of them were occupied by her sisters, Ksana demons like herself. Each had been fathered by the Isen Demon but they had come into this world by way of different mothers; mothers who had died during childbirth. The babies those chosen women had delivered were deadly poisonous as they came into the world, and not one of those mothers had survived.

And now, after years of living without a true knowledge of who and what they were—without knowing exactly what they were meant to be and do—the Ksanas were poison once again. As they became women they discovered the true depths of their varied powers. They also came into their own as the most deadly of all the demon daughters. No man could withstand their kiss.

The fourth bed in this large chamber was empty, awaiting yet another sister, perhaps.

One of Princess's sisters, the one called Divya, sat up in her bed. The other slept on. Perhaps her more limited powers did not allow her to see what Princess and Divya had seen.

"She has been awakened," Divya whispered.

Princess looked at her sister, seeing her well even in the dark. Divya was slighter in build than she or their other sister. Her blond hair was almost silver. "It was inevitable." Princess attempted to sound as if she didn't care. "She will come for us…in time. That was always meant to be." The witch and the blade. Separately they were mere annoyances. Separately they were nothing. Together…together they could ruin it all. One woman, one man. It was so unfair.

"One witch and one man," Divya said, sounding more annoyed than frightened. "Columbyana has many witches and more men than I can count, so I don't see what all the fuss is about."

"The witch will be hard to kill as long as the blade lives," Princess said. She was not afraid; not really. "We do not know the extent of her abilities, and he gives her strength. But the blade is just a man. Take him, and she will be just another witch, more easily disposed of if she dares to get in our way."

"Now that the witch has been awakened, we will be able to sense her," Divya said. "Perhaps we can dispose of her before she comes into her full power."

"Perhaps." Princess left her bed and walked to the window, bare feet on a cold floor, and looked down. She felt the moonlight wash over her, as powerful and energizing as sunlight. The night was hers, or soon would be. She still had so much to learn; there was so much to be taken from the world.

She would not let two pitiful humans get in her way. Joined or not, prophesied or not, witch or not…they were only human and should be easy enough to kill. The witch, the blade…perhaps both of them, just to be safe. She could not allow them to get in the way of what she wanted.

"Princess" was a start, but one day…one day she would be more than a Princess. Empress? Queen? Goddess? Her life, her rule, had only just begun.

Chapter Five

The final peal of the midnight bells faded away. Lyssa held onto Blade, who was moving in and out of her at a slow, steady pace. There had been some pain at first, but she could not say she felt pain any longer. A little discomfort, maybe. Mainly it was just odd to have a part of a man inside her. Odd and strangely compelling. Her hips moved against him, almost without thought or intent, as if she had an itch and he was scratching it gently. Gently. Oh, not *always* gently.

She'd known what to expect, in a vague way, but his manly part was bigger than she'd thought it would be. She hadn't gotten a good look at it, because it was so dark here in the shadows, but she could certainly feel it. And it was so *hard*. How did he keep that thing under control at all times? How on earth did any man walk down the street without waddling? She would have to ask Blade how he handled normal activities with such an impediment, but now was not the time for such a question.

How desperate she must be not to become a nun, to allow herself to be here, in this position, with this man she'd just met. Blade Renshaw was her husband, yes, but she didn't know him at all. Well, she knew that he was kind enough to rescue a woman in need, even though he didn't *look* at all kind. She knew he had no real desire to take a wife, though he didn't seem to mind this part of the arrangement at all. He had once been a sailor and a ship builder, he'd said, so why did he no longer live by the sea?

She knew he was most likely a thief, perhaps a beggar, perhaps both, but he'd spoken to Father Kiril as if he were a gentleman.

She really could not think of Father Kiril now! He would be shocked to see her in such an undignified position. She was shocked herself. This was certainly not how she'd imagined the night ending. She'd imagined a proper bed, one candle on the bedside table, some kissing before and after. Instead she was…here. And what was happening *here* had completely scattered her wits.

The important thing was that she was married and bedded, albeit without the bed. She was a wife in all ways. Maybe she didn't know much about the man she'd wed, but she had taken a husband before her twenty-third birthday. She wouldn't live her life alone in darkness, as her dreams—and that awful witch Vellance—had warned.

Her thoughts came quickly, disjointed. She really needed to stop thinking so much. The movement of her husband within her was terribly distracting, and soon she couldn't think of anything else but the way it felt *there*, where their bodies came together. She shifted, and he thrust deeper. She buried her face against his warm neck and breathed in his manly scent. It was intriguing; intoxicating.

Her body warmed, and her breath came differently, as if she had to work to bring air into her lungs. She forgot everything but the way it felt to have Blade inside her. She even forgot that she was in an alley, with her back against a rough wall and her skirt bunched up around her waist.

Blade moved faster, and so did she. It was as if she was driven instinctively to take him in. To rub her body against his and urge him deeper. She wanted more, but she wasn't sure exactly how to get it or even what *it* was. He drove deep and held himself still, and he shook. She felt his release inside her own body, heard a low groan in her ear. He went still, but for the effort it took for him to breathe. His body remained linked to hers, though it was now...different.

"Sorry," he said, as he withdrew and very gently placed her on her feet.

Reality came back to her as she smoothed out her skirt. Her body throbbed, her head swam, and she found herself...squirming. She wasn't exactly sure why.

"Why are you sorry? The fucking was not entirely unpleasant, and we are truly man and wife, as I requested. You have nothing to apologize for that I can see."

There was little light in the alleyway but there was enough for her to see that his lips twitched, as if there was a danger he might actually smile. "One day you *will* see," he said, straightening his clothes and then hers, though she'd already made an attempt at the chore. "I imagine. And, dear wife, I would suggest that you not use the word 'fuck' so frequently."

"Why not?" she asked. "You used the word yourself, so I assumed it was the proper word for what we just did. Did I not use the word correctly? Was my pronunciation incorrect?"

"Your pronunciation was stellar," Blade said, a touch of humor in his deep voice. "However, it is not a word used by proper ladies. Your Father Kiril would have heart failure if he heard you say it."

She inhaled sharply. "It's vulgar?"

"It is."

"You should have told me so immediately," she admonished.

"I suppose I should have," he admitted. He sounded much more agreeable than he had on their first meeting a short while ago, or even at the wedding, when he'd been so pleasant for Father Kiril's benefit. In fact, he sounded downright pleased with himself. "I'm surprised you don't know the word. It's rather common."

She hesitated to tell him that her father had always protected her from the more common aspects of life.

"You can use that word when we're alone," he said before she had a chance to prepare a response. "I rather like the sound of it coming out of your sweet, pretty mouth. You can whisper it into my ear whenever the mood strikes you."

"I can't see how that will be necessary," Lyssa said, as Blade took her arm and led her from the alley.

"Many pleasant things are not necessary, wife."

Wife. Hmm. She rather liked the way *that* word sounded coming out of *his* mouth.

They walked a short way down the road in silence. Lyssa deemed herself to be badly in need of a bath. The act of consummating her marriage had left her sweaty and sticky, and she was quite certain she smelled. She also felt as if Blade was still inside her, in a way she could not explain. Even though she had managed to get everything she wanted and needed on this momentous evening, she was horribly on edge, jumpy…skittish. And she was also convinced for some reason that they were not finished.

"Will we live in your room or in mine?" he asked.

Lyssa pursed her lips. What was done was done, but she hadn't yet worked out all the details. "I suppose we will live together eventually, but…"

"Not eventually," Blade said. "Immediately. How else am I to gain your father's trust so that he will take me into the palace with him on his next delivery?"

"There are many deliveries to be made in the coming months. It doesn't have to be the next."

"Yes, it does." He grabbed her shoulders and spun her about to face him. "I've waited too long. I won't wait any longer."

She wished she could see him better, but there was not enough light here. Not *nearly* enough light. "Why exactly do you wish to get into the palace?" she asked. She'd thought maybe he was just curious. There were many who simply wanted to see the imperial opulence for themselves, to walk among the fine ladies and gentlemen there, and look upon the jewels and paintings and sculptures. Perhaps he wanted a close look at the emperor, the empress, and their children. But as little as she knew about her husband, she seriously doubted that he was curious about such things. "You're not going in there to steal something, are you?" she asked, horrified.

"No."

"I know you're not above thievery," she argued. "The uniform you're wearing proves that much."

"I swear to you that I have no plans to steal anything from the palace."

That was a relief. She wanted no part in thievery.

"So, your room or mine?" he asked again.

Lyssa's mind spun. "Tonight I'll return to my house alone. My parents will be alarmed if they awake in the morning and I'm not there. They would also be shocked to find a man in my bed. I can only imagine the commotion that would ensue. It would be best if you came to the house later in the day, at which time I will make proper introductions."

"I suppose that will work. And then?"

A witch's prediction, a string of bad luck, and years of nightmares had spurred her to this point. But there was more. She didn't want to be a burden to her parents; she didn't want to be underfoot when the new baby arrived.

She certainly didn't want her father and her stepmother to look at her with pity because she couldn't find a husband and make a home of her own.

And she wanted her own home, at least for a while. She and Blade might not have the time she'd planned to have with her husband. If they lived in her father's house…No, even if it was a hovel, she *would* have her own home.

"We will live in your room."

"You haven't even asked what the place is like. What if you find it unsuitable?"

"No matter what your living circumstances may be, we will manage. You're much too tall for my bed. Kyran, the man I was supposed to marry this afternoon, isn't much taller than I am, so it would not have been an issue, but you simply will not *fit*. Yes, your room," she said with a determined nod of her head. No matter where it might be, it would surely not be as dark as the inside of a tomb or as quiet as a nunnery where everyone had taken a vow of silence, and no matter how unsuitable it was, she would not be living there alone.

Blade watched Lyssa walk carefully and quietly through the door to her small but more than satisfactory home. Though he could not see anything of the interior from where he stood, he was certain it was much nicer than the room he rented by the day, even though that rough room was much better than most of the places he'd slept in the past four years.

Lyssa would soon regret marrying him. But not before she served her purpose and got him into the palace.

He'd sunk to new lows in order to do what had to be done, but that realization that did not make him regret his decisions. It wasn't as if Lyssa got nothing out of the deal. She had the husband she'd been so desperate for, and the deed had been done before midnight. Who was he to say that her reasoning was invalid? He would make sure she wasn't entirely sorry before he finished his business here.

He and his wife would lie together again, and he would show her what pleasure could be had when a man and a woman came together. *Not entirely unpleasant*, she had said. She had no idea...and it would not be a sacrifice on his part to teach her.

Late as it was, as unexpectedly satisfied as he was, he didn't feel like sleeping. It wouldn't be the first sleepless night he'd passed. Nor the last. He walked past the tavern where he'd left his half-empty bottle of whisky sitting unattended. It would be long gone, and while there was more to be had, he did not want to dull his senses. Not now.

He kept walking. This was an unsavory part of town, and he passed more than one other tavern along the way, and also a rutting couple or two. Drunk and totally without shame, they did not even bother to slip into an alley, not at this late hour.

Not far beyond one loud and ill-kept tavern, he passed the two-story inn where he'd been renting a room, and as he watched a rail-thin prostitute and her customer fumbling with one another near the front entrance, he knew he could not bring Lyssa here. Even though he and his bride had just engaged in a very similar activity...it wasn't the same, not in his mind or in hers.

He'd sworn he would not accept help from anyone, he'd vowed to do this on his own, but that wouldn't be the first vow he'd broken—not even the first on this long day. At least this time he had a somewhat noble cause.

Besides, improved living conditions would instill confidence in Lyssa's father, who would be more willing to take his new son into the family business if he proved that he could care for her properly.

Perhaps his reasons were not so noble after all.

It was hours after he'd left Lyssa, and the sky was gray with morning light, when he knocked on a solid door far from the seedier section of town where he'd been spending his time since arriving in Arthes. He didn't have to wait long before the knock was answered.

Blade looked down on a face he knew well. The expression there flitted from anger to confusion and finally to something that might have been relief.

"I need your help."

Lyssa slept, and for the first time in a long while she did not dream at all. Instead of waking with a start and a scream, she stretched slowly, sighed, then burrowed in the blankets for a few precious moments.

She was married. A smile crossed her face. Perhaps it was not a real marriage, the way marriages were supposed to be, but she'd found a way around the old witch's grim prediction and averted disaster. She would be Bad Luck Lyssa no more. Take *that*, Vellance.

As she lay there, after a few hours of deep, undisturbed sleep, she imagined the day ahead of her. Introducing Blade to her parents was going to be tricky. "I sneaked out of the house last night and married a stranger" was not going to go over well.

It was bad enough that they would find the unkempt man unsatisfactory, but if she explained how he'd come to her rescue last night in the tavern…then she would have to explain how she'd come to be in that tavern in the first place.

That had not been the wisest decision she'd made in her twenty-three years, but in the end…in the end…

In the end she'd found herself coupling in an alleyway with a stranger. Her husband, yes, but still a man she did not know. So why did the thought of those few moments of fumbling and physical connection make her insides heavy and itchy? Why did the memory of Blade Renshaw making her his wife cause her to squirm in her own bed?

"Perhaps because it is long past time you were made a wife, Lyssa Tempest," she said softly as she sat up. No, not Tempest. She was now Lyssa *Renshaw*.

She washed, dressed, and presented herself for the morning meal with a smile on her face. While Sinmora made tea, Lyssa toasted yesterday's bread over the fire. What she needed to do was arrange for Blade to have a bath and a new suit of clothes before she introduced him to her father and stepmother. Preferably a clean outfit that had not been stolen. Many men wore beards, but his was desperately in need of a trim. She wondered if he would allow her to cut his hair. She found herself humming a merry tune and turned to find her stepmother staring at her.

"Are you all right, dear?"

"It's my birthday," Lyssa said. "Can I not be happy?"

"Of course you can." There was a fair amount of suspicion in those words.

Her father was as suspicious about her good mood as Sinmora had been, but somewhere between his toast and the dried figs, he apparently decided to accept his good fortune with a smile. In the past, there had been at least a week of self-pity and tears after a failed wedding.

They didn't know that she'd beaten the prophecy, that she *was* a wife.

How to tell them, though…Not a single scenario seemed right. And really, why should she rush to tell them anything? While there had been a deadline on the marriage itself, sharing the news of that marriage could be done at any time, she supposed. Not that she was a coward, but such important news should be delivered in just the right way.

As she often did, Lyssa opened the store along with her father. The shop was next door to their home, and while it was small and always had been, Cyrus Tempest was known for offering fine goods at reasonable prices. Business had been slow lately, she admitted, thanks to a new merchant setting up shop in town, but so far they had managed to meet their needs. Still, with her own troubles behind her, she could see the worry on his face. He looked older, more haggard, and she felt guilty for getting so wrapped up in her own troubles that she hadn't seen what was going on at home.

Was he worried about the baby, or had the decrease in business hurt more than he'd let on?

Surely he would welcome the news of her marriage, as he had welcomed the news of a baby. Life would go on as it should. She would do what she could to help his business and then she could start a new life knowing that he, and her stepmother and her brother or sister, were well off and happy.

And she…well, one step at a time.

Shortly after opening, Edine Lair—Lyssa's greatest friend in the world—stepped into the shop, a baby on her hip, a toddler's fat little hand clutched in hers. With child again, she never seemed tired or frustrated, no matter how hectic her life seemed to be. Her dark hair shone and was held perfectly in place. Her skin always had a fresh, healthy glow. As she walked into the shop, Edine caught Lyssa's eye and grinned widely.

"I'm so sorry I missed the wedding! Yesterday was impossibly hectic." Her easy smile widened. "And where is the lucky groom this morning?"

I have no idea....

Lyssa's father groaned; Edine's smile died quickly.

"Not again," Edine said. "Lyssa!" She glanced around the small store, making sure there were no customers present to overhear. "What happened this time?"

"Kyran left me for a woman he met on the road." The words didn't hurt the way they had yesterday. She didn't feel hate for Kyran or for the woman who had stolen his heart. She'd never loved him and he had never loved her, so his heart had been available for stealing, she supposed.

"Oh, no!" Edine rushed toward Lyssa. "And today is the day. You're twenty-three! It's too late!" Of all her friends, Edine had been the biggest believer in the prophecy. She had always been Lyssa's most loyal supporter, the one shoulder available for crying upon when a potential groom died or ran off.

Like many Columbyanans, Edine was afraid of magic. Witches terrified her. In the minds of many, there was little difference in the powers of a witch—whether she declared herself good or bad—and those of the evil Isen Demon. After the war with that demon, many had turned their backs on magic altogether. Edine among them.

Edine shifted the baby and released the toddler's hand to give Lyssa a hug. The hugs were not what they had once been, thanks to the baby and the huge belly and the fact that the eldest child took the opportunity of his newfound freedom to run toward a display of carved wooden boxes. He knew some of them played music.

Lyssa was getting ready to rush after him when she saw her father step in and intercept the child, lifting him with a smile.

He beamed at the boy, much happier than he'd been just moments earlier. The worry seemed to melt from his face, along with several of the years etched there. Perhaps he was already imagining his own son.

"I'm all right, truly," Lyssa said, reassuring her friend. "What will be, will be." She was anxious to tell Edine all about Blade, but not before she told her parents. And goodness knows the questions she wanted to ask her friend were not ones she could put forth in front of her father. A woman-to-woman talk was most definitely in order, and soon.

"That awful *awful* witch!" Edine whispered harshly.

Before the conversation could continue, the door opened, and all eyes shifted in the direction of the entrance. Lyssa's heart took a strange little flip. Edine sighed, softly enough but in a manner totally unsuited to a happily married woman with two children and another on the way. The man who entered the shop was tall, and his raven black hair was pulled away from a strong face and back into a long, neat braid. He was clean shaven, with a proper chin and a nicely sharp jawline. He was not pretty, not at all, but his face was masculine and very nicely arranged, she had to admit. It was a man's face, strong and…interesting. His suit was plain, but well made of fine material; his boots were polished. There was something intriguing about the way he moved, with strength and a masculine grace that spoke to the woman in her.

Why could she not have met *him* last night?

As that thought crossed her mind he looked at her and squinted a bit, narrowing his gaze like a hawk honing in on its prey. With a start she recognized those eyes. No other man had eyes like those, brilliant blue and disturbing. She *had* met him last night. This intriguing, handsome man was her husband.

Chapter Six

Blade watched as recognition dawned on his wife's face. Recognition and surprise. She was so easy to read. It was if every thought that passed through her brain was instantly transferred to her face. Only an honest person could be so open. He hadn't known anyone truly honest in a very long time.

Once Lyssa's surprise passed, she began to panic. She didn't squeal or jump up and down, but that panic was visible in her eyes and the flushing of her cheeks, and in the way her delicate fingers fluttered. She didn't move, other than those fingers, and she didn't say a word. She looked as if she wanted to screech, but she did not. Obviously she hadn't told her father—a busy man who stood just a few feet away—about her marriage, then. She looked Blade in the eye and shook her head quickly, barely moving it side to side.

By the light of day, last night's plan must seem foolish to her. They were married, she was well and truly his wife. Still, perhaps she wasn't prepared to proceed as they had planned. He read her expression, seeing all too clearly that as she stood there and stared, wide-eyed, she was formulating yet another plan in her mind.

It would be easy enough to fabricate a brief courtship, then go through yet another wedding ceremony, one her parents could be a part of. He imagined that would be preferable, from Lyssa's point of view, to simply announcing that they were married and then taking on the questions about the hows and the whys.

But he no longer had the time for such a game. He'd learned just that morning that Volker would soon be traveling to Tryfyn to meet with their Foreign Minister. If he didn't move fast, he would lose this opportunity.

Lyssa stepped toward him quickly, her chin up, her eyes bright. She was even prettier by the light of day than she had looked last night, well-rested and not nearly as worried as she'd been then. She shook her head again, so slightly no one but he could see the movement, as she stopped directly before him. Her eyes widened a bit more when they met his. He half expected her jaw to drop. She was still surprised.

That he was here, or that he knew how to shave?

"Mr. Renshaw, isn't it?" she asked politely.

Since he needed her assistance, he decided that he had no choice but to play along. For now. "Yes, *Miss* Tempest."

Lyssa turned her pretty head and smiled at her father. "Mr. Renshaw stopped by last week when you were out helping Sinmora with the delivery from the butcher. He's interested in some fabrics, but he didn't care for what we have in stock, and I told him we wouldn't have anything new until later this week." She looked at Blade again. "I'm afraid the shipment has not yet arrived."

The explanation seemed unnecessary to him, but no one else seemed to wonder about it. He glanced around and saw the display of fabric at the back of the store. "Perhaps I will look again at what you have in stock. Would you care to help me, Miss Tempest?" He walked toward the rear of the shop, where there would be some distance and a crowded shelf or two between them and her father.

"Of course," she responded brightly.

When they had almost reached the display of fabric, he turned and stared down at her, narrowing his eyes. Like it or not, he remembered too vividly taking her against a wall, making her a wife in the most basic of ways. The memory was a strong one. He wanted her again. In a bed. Naked. Lit candles all around so he could see all of her. And he wouldn't leave her wanting next time.

But that wasn't why he was here.

"I take it you did not tell your father that you and I were married last night." He kept his voice low.

Lyssa shook her head. "I couldn't. I thought and thought, but there is no reasonable explanation. How could I tell my father that I ran out of the house after he retired for the night and married a complete stranger I found in a tavern I should never have set foot in?"

"Perhaps in just those words. It is the truth, after all."

She pursed her lips, glancing to the side as if she no longer wanted to look at him. "I have a better idea," she whispered, and then her voice rose to a pitch no one in the store could possibly miss. "Why, I would be delighted to take a stroll with you, Mr. Renshaw." She paused for a moment. "Sunset? Lovely. I'll see you then." She lowered her voice again. "Stop by the church and tell Father Kiril to keep last night's ceremony to himself for the moment. Promise him more money for the roof if he objects. He is a man of God, but he also has a great liking for coin, and the building does *desperately* need a new roof."

Just as he had suspected. She had a new plan, a game to play. He leaned down close. "Of course, my dear. Whatever you desire, you have only to ask." For a moment their eyes met and held. For years, he'd wanted nothing more than revenge. No, not revenge. *Justice.* But for a moment, for an unexpected split second of time, he wanted something else even more than he wanted Volker.

Her.

Delivering a basket of fruit, tobacco, and candies to the elderly Madam Azar took Lyssa past the palace. As she walked the streets of Arthes—past stone houses as much green as gray, thanks to healthy vines; past a smattering of brightly colored doors, red, blue, and green; past neighbors she recognized and those she did not; past the stone palace, well guarded and an impressive ten stories tall, with two additional levels below ground—her mind was on a dozen matters, not the least of which was what she might wear tonight when Blade escorted her on a romantic stroll. She normally wore clothing that wouldn't call unnecessary attention to herself. Dull colors, simple cuts, no frills or bows. Being called Bad Luck Lyssa for years was embarrassing enough without intentionally drawing the attention of those she passed. *Who is that? Oh, yes, Bad Luck Lyssa…Terrible Tempest…Don't look her in the eye or you might drop dead on the spot….*

Her wardrobe was not extensive, but she had a few good frocks to call her own. They were all brown, drab green, or faded plum. Perhaps a colorful scarf and a flower in her hair would brighten the ensemble enough to make a difference. Why on earth she cared about impressing Blade Renshaw she did not know. They were already married. He was a temporary solution to her problem. She barely knew him.

But last night, for a few minutes, she had known him very well. Thinking about those minutes, reliving them, was unusually enjoyable. She could almost feel guilty for having these unexpected feelings, but she did not. Blade was, after all, her husband. Even if just for a while. She wondered if they would join again as man and wife, perhaps in a bed this time.

Why did she feel as if taking him as her husband had changed her in some elemental way? In a matter of minutes, he had awakened a part of her that she hadn't known existed. She was a woman now, but...why was she so certain the change went deeper than that? Perhaps relieving the worry about being forever on her own was enough to make her feel this way. Stronger, prettier. Near giddy, if she were to be honest with herself.

Suddenly her mind cleared as if a strong gust of wind had whipped through and wiped out all thought, and she spun around to face the palace. Her gaze was drawn up and up until it landed on a window of the level just below the top. Level Two. No one lived there, not anymore. Those higher rooms were used for storage, or at least that was what she had been told.

But they were not empty now. She knew it as surely as she knew her name was Lyssa Renshaw. And what waited there, high above the ground, was not good. Not good at all. Darkness dwelled beyond that window. The kind of darkness a witch had used to frighten a young Lyssa years ago. Evil, and somehow that evil was looking at her the same way she was looking at it.

Not it, *her.* Lyssa's spine tingled; the tiny hairs on her arms and the back of her neck stood and danced. A strong breeze rose up out of nowhere and hit her in the face, and she smelled rain in that breeze. Rain and lightning. She could almost hear the thunder, though above the sky was clear and blue.

She shook off the strange feelings that had come over her and spun about, forcing herself to turn away from the palace. The wind—had it been real or imagined?—died. The past couple of days had been much too exciting, and her mind was playing tricks on her. That was the only explanation. Time to get back to what was really important. What to wear.

Not darkness, not evil. Those were thoughts for another woman, not her. Not Lyssa Renshaw.

Madam Azar met Lyssa at the door, as she always did. Her legs were not as strong as they had once been, but her hazel eyes were bright, and she had a good mind. Her late husband had been an assistant to some minister or another for many years. One of her sons had taken to the sea, the other...well, no one knew where the other was. He had always been a bit of a wastrel.

"Lyssa, you are positively glowing!" Madam Azar said with a wide smile. She still had all her teeth, but they were crooked and stained. The tobacco was for her own use, after all. "Marriage agrees with you." With that, the older woman winked.

Hiding the strange feelings that wink aroused in her, Lyssa stepped inside the house and carried the basket to the table, focusing her thoughts on the task at hand and dismissing her earlier imaginings about evil in the emperor's palace.

Madam Azar and her husband had once lived in a fine home on another street, but since his death she'd lived here, in a cottage not even as large as the one Lyssa shared with her father and Sinmora. The older woman said it suited her to live in a place where she did not see her husband in every corner, where she could live her new life as a widow and not be haunted by the past.

She rarely left this house.

After taking a deep breath for courage, Lyssa said, "I am sorry to say, my groom ran off with another woman."

"Not again," Madam Azar whispered. "Oh, my dear."

"It was rather upsetting at the time, but I'm fine now, really." Lyssa smiled.

Madam Azar wrinkled her brow. "You *do* look different, though, I swear it. Brighter. Happier. I would almost swear something momentous has occurred."

Was she so transparent? Did others see the change she felt? It would be easy to tell the old woman the truth: that she'd found another husband quite by chance. That she was well wed and no longer a virgin, and didn't mourn the loss of groom number four at all. But not until she'd told her father. Even if it was unlikely that the old woman would step foot outside her door, even if she had no one to tell, it just wouldn't be right.

"No. Nothing has changed." She sounded *quite* convincing, at least to her own ears.

Madam Azar sat and began to sift through her purchases. As she did, Lyssa's eyes were drawn to an odd spot on the woman's knee. She reached forward, then pulled her hand back, uncertain. What she saw—or thought she saw—was surely an illusion of some kind, a trick of the light. But the spot was very strange. It was not on the fabric that covered the knee but seemed to float above like a small bit of misplaced, dense fog. Yellowy and greenish, and flitting about as if daring Lyssa to snatch it up.

First Level Two and now this! She was losing her mind.

She tried to convince herself that she didn't see anything at all, but the green mist continued to dance. Finally, unable to help herself, Lyssa reached out and clasped her hand over that knee. Her fingers tightened there of their own accord. The spot disappeared, perhaps had never existed to begin with, and yet she did not let go. The flesh beneath the heavy fabric was hot, then cold, then warm and normal.

Madam Azar jumped a bit and stared at Lyssa, as she finally lifted her hand away. "What was that about?"

Lyssa glanced down at her hand. It looked no different than it had before, but it *felt* very different. Cold fire; that was what she felt on the palm of her hand. *Cold fire.* Her palm tingled for a moment, and then the sensation faded. "I thought I saw a spider on your knee, but I guess it was just a trick of the light." A small lie seemed a better response than the confusing truth.

Madam Azar reached for her purse, which was sitting on the table, and withdrew the coins to pay for her goods. She counted them out, one at a time, and then handed over a list for the next delivery. Then she stood to escort Lyssa back to the door. She took one step and stopped, gasping.

"I can show myself out," Lyssa said, reaching out to assist the woman back to her chair. "You should not hurt yourself...."

"It's not that," the old woman said. "In fact, quite the opposite. My knee has bothered me for years, and there are times when I'm just sure it won't support my weight, but right now there is no pain." She stared hard at Lyssa. "None at all. The knee you touched, there where you thought you saw a spider, it doesn't hurt anymore."

"All pains come and go, do they not?" Lyssa said. That was the only possible explanation, the only logical reason for Madam Azar's knee to be so much better than it had been just moments earlier.

"Yes, but..."

"You sit and rest." Lyssa placed her hands on the old woman's bony shoulders. "I'll be back at the end of the week with your next delivery."

"Yes," Madam Azar whispered. "I will enjoy the respite while it lasts."

Lyssa smiled, though she did not feel at all like smiling. She left the house in a hurry, and once she was outside she stopped, leaned against the door and closed her eyes. Three deep breaths, then she opened her eyes and looked down at the palm of her hand. It still looked no different, the sensation of cold fire had gone, and yet…something *was* different.

All she wanted, all she had *ever* wanted, was a normal life. An ordinary life. And yet at every turn she was faced with obstacles. The curse, the dreams, the lost grooms, Blade…and now this.

What was happening to her?

Chapter Seven

Blade fought for patience. He had no time for courting. He did not have a spare minute to waste pretending that he was someone he was not. And yet here he was, strolling along the streets of Arthes as if he didn't have a care in the world beyond wooing the pretty woman at his side.

Knowing that Volker would be leaving Arthes in a few weeks didn't change his plans, but he now had to deal with the issue of time. He could not—would not—wait.

The demon daughters, born during and just after the war with the Isen Demon, were a bone of contention in an otherwise peaceful country. Some Columbyanans thought the half-demons should all be executed the moment they were identified. Others had qualms about putting fifteen- and sixteen-year-old girls—pretty and innocent-looking young women, for the most part—to death. It had been proven that some of them were more human than demon, that some of them could be, *should be*, saved. But who made the decisions, and what happened when those decisions were wrong? Was it preferable to put an innocent to death or to allow a monster to live?

Since many of the children had fled to Tryfyn, that country now faced the same problem, and according to the man who'd informed Blade of Volker's plans—unintentionally sharing important information over beer and a meat pie—that was the reason for the upcoming journey. As if a handful of over-fed, pampered appointed officials could put their heads together and come up with a solution.

His own goal was smaller. Simpler. Clearer. He needed only to avenge one little girl. He cared nothing about the rest.

Volker would be much too heavily protected on the road; Blade had already discovered as much. That meant he had little time to make himself a part of Lyssa's family and enter the palace as a seemingly harmless merchant. Hell, he'd tried everything else. Everything but an all out attack that would endanger not only Volker but those around him. He could not allow any innocents to be caught in the crossfire. He might have done murder in the past, but he'd only sent those who truly deserved death into the Land of the Dead.

"If we are going to be man and wife, even temporarily, then I should know more about you," Lyssa said as if their evening stroll was nothing more than it appeared to be. "Where are you from? Is Blade the name your mother gave you, or is it a nickname because you're so good with a knife or a sword? Do you have brothers and sisters? Are your parents living?"

"I've told you all you need to know about me," he answered curtly.

"You've told me practically nothing," she said, and while she sounded a bit peeved, she was far from angry. He looked down at her. Lyssa was short, her steps were not long enough to suit him, and she was slightly built. Fragile, even. A print scarf had been wrapped around her shoulders, but other than that the outfit she wore might almost have been chosen for its lack of color. Unlike the friend who had been in her father's shop earlier in the day, unlike the other young women he saw walking on this evening, she did not dress to call attention to herself.

But when she looked up at him and narrowed her eyes, he saw power there. Power and beauty. Not just in her glare, but in her entire body. At first glance she might be a perfectly ordinary woman, but if one were to look long and hard enough…

"You know more about me than I know about you," he said. "You go first."

She nodded once. He wasn't off the hook, he knew, but he had managed to wrangle a reprieve.

"I have always lived in Arthes. My father is a shopkeeper, as you know. My mother died when I was very young. I don't remember her at all. When I was ten, my father married Sinmora. She's been a good stepmother, I must say. Better than some I have met. My friend Aria has the most hideous stepmother…but you don't care about that, I suppose." She glanced up at him, and she smiled. "I suspect I look like my mother, because I look nothing at all like my father. Except for the hair. It's the same color, or was before his began to turn gray and fall out. He has no painting of my mother, not even a sketch, though he said she had blond hair and blue eyes, and I don't, so I can't be sure I look like her. You know about the witch I met when I was fifteen, and how she said…well, you know what she said."

She was talking so fast there was barely a chance for Blade to interrupt. But he did. "And you believed this witch."

Lyssa became unnaturally quiet. Her lips thinned a bit, as she considered her answer, and then she almost pouted. He could not help but note that she had soft lips, full and lush and perfectly colored. He'd been inside her, but he had not kissed her. As he looked at her mouth he was reminded that he had not kissed a woman for a very long time.

"Not at first," she finally answered. "But she was very scary and convincing, and when I had so much trouble getting a groom to the altar, and…"

Something about the way she paused, the way she held her breath, prodded him to say, "And?"

"It's not important," she said reluctantly, in a tone that made it very clear that what she had *not* said was much more important than what she'd shared.

"Humor me."

She stopped. There was little activity in this part of the city at this time of the day, so no one was watching, not that he could see. She faced him, tilted her chin up bravely and said, "Dreams. I had…dreams."

"A dream is the reason you married a complete stranger and lifted your skirt in an—"

Lyssa lifted a hand to silence him. "We will not discuss that. It's done and forgotten." She looked away and blushed deeply. Their quick tryst in the alleyway had not been forgotten at all. Not by her and certainly not by him. "And to answer your question, it was not a dream. It was *dreams*. Many of them. All of them frightening and dark and…and in them I was always alone, and I knew that to be alone was wrong. Who wants to be alone? No one."

She would be alone when he was dead. Not only alone, but the widow of an assassin. Would she be punished for his crimes? Would the emperor blame his wife? After all the time he'd spent getting to this place, he shouldn't care.

But he did.

He couldn't. She was a means to an end and nothing more. She would get him into the palace so he could finish what had begun four years ago.

Only four years? It seemed longer. It seemed as if his entire life had been spent avenging Runa. He'd barely survived the sword that had stopped him as he'd rushed toward her body. They'd left him for dead; he'd believed he *was* dead for a while. After he'd healed, it had taken more than a year to find out what had really happened, to identify those responsible and to reach this point where the last guilty man—the one who had wielded the sword that had killed his little sister—was right before him, just out of reach.

He could not afford to care what happened to Lyssa after he was gone.

Blade refused to tell her anything else about himself. He said he was on his own and didn't mind at all, repeated that he had once been a sailor and a boat builder…and that was it. There had to be more. He was an infuriating man in so many ways.

Infuriating and interesting. Though he had managed to scrounge up a nice suit of clothes, and had bathed and shaved and pulled his long hair back, he still looked more primitive than civilized. It was the eyes, she decided; ice blue and sharp and…ruthless. It was as if a storm lived in those eyes, as if they had seen more than any man should see and had been changed by it. And yet she was not afraid. She hadn't been afraid last night, either, not once he'd rescued her. She should be, she supposed, but instead she felt oddly comforted by his presence.

Again, she had the fleeting thought that he was much like the sword from her dream, her Blade. She should be afraid he would cut her, but she was not.

She'd always had good instincts about people. At least, she had good instincts about people she didn't intend to marry. Even her father said so. Her problem had always been trusting herself to listen to those instincts. After judging so poorly for so many years where a husband was concerned, how could she possibly rely on her own instincts?

Still, she was certain that Blade, for all his secrets, would never hurt her. She believed that to the depths of her soul. Then again she had also trusted groom number four...

"When will we tell your father that we're married?" he asked as they approached her home. The sun had set, and while a bit of light remained in the sky, it would soon be dark.

"Soon," she said.

"Tonight?"

"Perhaps not *that* soon. We can court a while, then have another wedding. Something appropriate and...not so rushed."

They stopped in front of the door. He took her shoulders in his big hands and stepped close. Very close. "I suspected you might have something like that in mind. I have made suitable living arrangements. We are married. Why not now?"

"It's just...my father needs time....I have to come up with a way to explain....And I don't know you nearly as well as I should. I don't even know how old you are. I have not yet inspected your living quarters and...and..." She sputtered to a halt. Good heavens, she had lost her mind. Her husband was standing too close to her, and she could barely breathe. Her heart was beating too hard and too fast, and she couldn't help but wonder what kind of living arrangements he'd made. He had bathed and shaved and dressed very nicely, but he was still the same man who'd made her his wife quickly and completely, just last night. The same man who had been inside her, who had made her feel things she had never expected to feel.

And when he ignored all her perfectly reasonable explanations about why they should wait and leaned in to press his hot mouth to the side of her neck, her knees went weak.

His mouth rested near her ear, and she felt his touch everywhere. From the top of her head to the toes that curled in her boots. The heat of his breath made her shiver. His closeness made her heart pound, and she was so tempted to grab him and pull him closer.

"Tell him we have fallen instantly and completely in love," Blade whispered, his voice deep and dark and smooth. He kissed her neck again in that same sensitive place, and she could not help but think of the way he had felt inside her last night. How he had filled her. How she had moved against him. Her knees trembled and threatened to give way. "Tell him you cannot live without me." With that he kissed her directly on the mouth, and for an instant she thought those words were absolutely right. She truly could not live without him. Without *this*.

He held her tight, slipped the tip of his tongue between her lips, and something in her came apart. She knotted her hands in his shirt. If he had not been holding her, she would have dropped to the ground. Her mind spun and her body shook. She wanted more. She wanted to see him naked, run her hands over his skin and press her naked body to his. She wanted him inside her again. She wanted to finish what had not yet been finished.

Her fears of being alone forever were gone, thanks to him. Maybe that was why she felt this way. He had saved her from her curse, and she was grateful. Floating, tingly, excited…and grateful.

Who was she kidding? Gratitude didn't make her heart beat this way, didn't awaken her senses and make her crave more. So much more. Did she really care how old he was?

If he had family? And so what if his room was small and as unkempt as he'd been last night?

"Stay right here," she said when Blade abruptly ended the kiss. She turned and opened the door to her home. Her father and stepmother were sitting at the dining table, talking. Maybe about the new baby, maybe about Bad Luck Lyssa and how they were going to be stuck with her for the rest of their lives. It no longer mattered. She beamed at them both.

"I'm married!"

When Blade had kissed his bride, he'd been trying to hurry things along. He did not have weeks to wait for her to decide how she wanted to share their news. He had no time to plan a proper wedding.

But he'd had no idea she would decide to blurt out the simplest version of the truth to her father and be done with it. Fortunately, after the initial shock, Cyrus Tempest had bought their story that they'd known one another for a short while and had fallen in love. There was no need to tell the man that his daughter had gone to a tavern to fetch a husband. Any husband.

The way Cyrus Tempest looked at his daughter when Lyssa wasn't watching was curious. After they had stepped inside the house to offer a bit more detail about their situation, Lyssa had glanced up at Blade as if she really were…thrilled. In that instant, Tempest had looked relieved, concerned, and more than a bit befuddled. When Lyssa had faced her father once more, his expression was once again settled. Still. Emotionless. Something odd was going on. Then again, perhaps it was simply Lyssa's bad history with potential grooms that caused her father's strange mix of emotions.

His wife's relationship with her father was not his concern. He was one step closer to Volker, and nothing else mattered.

The news shared, Lyssa had packed a small bag and together they'd set out for their new home. Side by side, in soft twilight, they walked to a very nice part of town where the houses were larger and the streets were wider. The way Lyssa looked up and around at the homes here, the joy on her face, made Blade glad he'd made suitable arrangements.

When they reached their destination Blade took his wife's arm and led her up a narrow but well landscaped walk. Their host was watching for them, and opened the door before they had a chance to knock. Standing in the doorway of one of the nicer homes in Arthes, Blade made introductions.

"Lyssa, dear, this is Hagan Elmar."

"Oh, I know Mister Elmar very well." Lyssa offered a quick but proper curtsy. "He's a good customer of my father's."

"Hagan and my mother were once great friends," Blade explained. "He has kindly allowed me to rent his guest house."

The years had not been especially kind to Hagan. He was short and round, so round he was about to pop the buttons of his jacket, as he invited them to step inside. He'd lost most of his hair, hanging onto only a few stubborn white tufts, and where once there had been a strong chin there were now many. But his eyes still sparked with intelligence, and his smile was genuine.

"My son lived in the guest house for many years," Hagan said, "but he's recently moved east with his wife. I will be more than happy to have someone occupying the place. A house should be lived in." The older man had the decency not to mention that the suit Blade was wearing had also once belonged to his son.

Curiosity was more than apparent on Lyssa's face. Here was someone who could likely answer many of her questions about her husband's past. She would probably try to weasel as much information as possible from Hagan when the opportunity arose. Why she cared, he could not imagine. It wasn't as if they would be husband and wife for very long. Just long enough for her to get him into the palace.

Hagan had secrets of his own, so it was unlikely he would share Blade's.

They didn't stay in the main house for more than a few minutes. Lyssa thanked their host, and then Blade escorted Lyssa out the front door and around the side of the house, where another narrow stone walk led to their new home. Well-tended plants lined the walkway. Some bushes were in bloom, while others were dormant or sported tight, unopened buds. Lyssa took it all in, as if she had never seen a garden before.

The guest house was more than sufficient for their needs. In fact, it was larger than the house Lyssa had lived in with her parents. There was a spacious, well furnished main room, with a fireplace and several comfortable chairs. The kitchen and dining area was separated from the main room by a wall adorned with paintings. The single bedroom was large and luxurious, compared to the rough room Blade had been renting by the night.

It was a nice place and would make a good home for someone some day. He wondered if Hagan would allow Lyssa to remain here after he was dead. But asking, making those arrangements, would give too much away.

If Hagan knew why Blade was here, if he knew all that Blade had learned, would he insist on helping? Blade had not told the old man that he'd identified Runa's murderer, much less that the killer was a well-respected Minister living here in Arthes. Not many would believe—or care—but Hagan would. Blade was willing to give his own life to avenge Runa, but he would not ask anyone else to make the same sacrifice.

Not everyone would believe him if he told what he knew to be true, if he accused a highly placed Columbyana Minister of killing a child. And even if he did voice that accusation, there were those who would defend Volker's actions.

There were even those who would thank Volker for killing that child…and how many others? How many other little girls had Miron Volker killed?

What even Hagan didn't know, what no one but Blade had ever known with certainty, was that Runa Renshaw had been one of the Isen Demon's daughters.

Chapter Eight

Lyssa had only brought a few things with her from home: a change of clothes; the nightgown she was wearing now; her hairbrush and favorite soap. That was all she needed for tonight. She would collect the rest tomorrow.

Not that she had much to collect. She'd never been all that fond of jewelry. Anything on a chain—no matter how lightweight and pretty it might be—irritated her neck and made her feel as if she were choking. Rings and bracelets seemed to get in the way, catching on the fabrics in her father's shop. She had a nice pair of walking boots and two pairs of slippers, which was really more than she needed. She did love the newest slippers, she admitted to herself. A few well-made dresses. Rose-scented water. A few coins, those which she'd promised to Blade if he would escort her home. She had nothing of consequence to contribute to a new household, no pots or pans or linens.

She had almost married four times, and though she had always planned to live with her parents for a short while afterward, why had she never given any thought to equipping a household before now? In the back of her mind, had she realized…?

No. Impossible. She simply had not thought ahead. And since the cottage Blade had rented was very well stocked, it made little sense for her to worry about linens and pots now.

She'd thought that perhaps her father and stepmother would be shocked to find out she'd married a man they'd never met. A man they knew nothing about. She'd thought they might be concerned that she was leaving home with a stranger. But instead of being outraged, they'd been relieved. They'd tried to hide their reaction, but she'd seen that relief in their eyes. She'd felt that relief as if it had been a tangible thing she could reach out and touch.

She tried not to feel hurt. She made a real attempt to look at things in a more charitable light, especially when it came to the people she loved. Maybe they were simply happy for her, relieved that she at last had the husband she'd wanted for so long. Then again, maybe they were glad to be rid of her. She didn't blame them. With the new baby coming, it even made sense.

In spite of it all, Lyssa did believe that her father loved her. She'd never doubted that love at all, even though there were moments when she caught him looking at her as if she were a stranger wearing his daughter's skin. But he did love her, and he was understandably relieved to see her in a husband's care. After all, he needed to make more room in his life and his home for the son Sinmora carried.

Standing by the big bed in her new chamber, dressed in an ordinary nightgown that had seen better days, she somehow knew that the child Sinmora carried was a boy. A healthy boy who would be much like his father. She listened to the rain patter on the windows and the roof, and she could actually see the fat, pink little boy. They would be a happy family, and they did not need her underfoot.

Not long after she and Blade had shared a simple meal of cheese, bread, and fruit, clouds had rolled in. Darkness had already fallen, as they ate, but the heavy clouds dimmed the moonlight. The guest house windows had been opened wide and the air that wafted inside had smelled of rain; the same rain she'd smelled that afternoon as she'd stared up at

Level Two. A gust of wind had made the candles flicker, and had also made Lyssa shiver. Just a bit.

There was no reason for complaint or second thoughts. She'd gotten what she wanted. She was married, she had moved out of her childhood home, and she had beaten the deadline given to her by a toothless, scary witch by one full strike of the palace clock. So why did she feel more alone than ever at this moment? Maybe because no matter what the reason, her father *was* glad to be rid of her, and so was Sinmora. Her husband had married her for his own purposes, and love was not among them. She could not hold that against him since she had married him for her own purposes, but still...Heaven above, she did not know Blade Renshaw nearly well enough to call him husband.

The door opened and Lyssa jumped as Blade walked into the room. She'd seen him just a few moments ago, and yet again she was startled by his size and the coldness of his narrowed eyes. His gaze landed on the bed and lingered there for a moment.

Why did it seem that he sucked all the air out of a room when he entered it?

Finally he spoke. "I'll sleep on the floor in the main room. If there are extra blankets..."

Suddenly she was reminded that she was indeed *not* alone. Maybe she didn't know Blade well, but she would. In time. Her plan had been to use this man to beat the witch's prophecy, but at the moment she had no desire to replace him with another, more suitable, husband. When she looked at him she saw great potential. He was nice looking, stronger than most, a good kisser, and he had provided a very nice home. Her husband was a mystery to her still, and yet...He was hers. She knew that now. He was *hers*.

"No," Lyssa said softly. "The bed is a big one, more than large enough for both of us."

He took a step toward her. "If we sleep in that big bed together, we will end up fucking again. Maybe tonight, maybe tomorrow night, but I will not share a bed with you and pretend not to want you." Was he trying to scare her? If so, he failed miserably.

"I would like that." Lyssa felt herself blush. Though she fought for tight control, she didn't succeed. Not entirely. Was it proper behavior for a wife to be so bold? She couldn't be sure, but it didn't feel wrong to be honest and open with Blade. "We can…" Oh, now that she knew it was a bad word, she could not say it! "We can do what husbands and wives do, as we are, in fact, husband and wife."

Blade didn't have a particularly expressive face, and still he looked surprised by her words. Had he expected her to be shy or coy? Did he think she would hide under the covers and send him away to sleep on a cold, hard floor?

"This marriage is a temporary one. You've made that clear," he said. "If we share a bed you could find yourself with child," he added, and it sounded like a threat.

Was she ready for that? A baby? *His* baby? "Maybe I will and maybe I won't. That question is a part of life and it is certainly a part of any marriage, is it not?"

Besides, while she wasn't ready to say so aloud, joining with her husband had not been entirely unpleasant. In a bed, with a bit of light to see by, it might be downright enjoyable. Shouldn't she have a proper marital bedding? Something more appropriate than a quick tryst in a dark alleyway.

"I sleep naked," Blade said, and again his words sounded very much like a threat.

"Lovely." She took a deep breath, grabbed the hem of her nightgown and swiftly pulled it over her head. She dropped it to the floor. "Then so shall I." She sat on the side of the bed for a moment, then slipped her legs beneath the coverlet. It was perfectly naturally for her to be a little shy. No man had ever seen her naked!

For a few long moments Blade just looked at her. He looked and he looked. Finally he began to remove his own clothes. He did not rush, so she returned the favor and looked at *him*. Her first thought was that he was rather hairy, and big, and hard. Well, not too hairy, but there was hair on his chest, and lower, and she really did like that little dusting on his forearms. A scar marred the perfection of his chest, but her eyes did not linger there. There was so much beauty to look at, so much to study.

She was smooth—for the most part—and small and soft, so she found his physical makeup…fascinating. Utterly fascinating. She should be afraid to share a bed with a man so much larger and stronger than she. But she wasn't. She wasn't afraid at all.

She was glad of the rain. The sound was soothing, and it insulated them from the rest of the world somehow.

"I should turn around and walk away," he said beneath his breath, almost as if he were talking to himself.

She met his gaze, squinted a bit as he sometimes did and tilted her head to one side. "Why?"

Blade had wanted nothing more than revenge for so long that to want anything else seemed very wrong.

He wanted her. Maybe he'd wanted her from the moment he'd seen her walking blindly away from the palace with her father, afraid of the coming marriage that was not to be.

When he'd still been able to feel her, to smell her on his skin, he'd planned to show her what pleasure a man and wife could share. Only later, with some distance, had he begun to have doubts about the wisdom of that plan. When he was gone another man could teach her. Another man could share her bed. There was no reason for him to encourage the kind of closeness lying with her would create. And yet here he stood, unable to walk away.

She pointed. "How do you walk around all day with that…that…"

"Cock," he provided in a harsh tone.

Her eyes rose up to meet his. "That is another vulgar word, isn't it?"

"I suppose."

"Well, whatever it should be called, however do you manage?"

He could almost smile. Almost. Here was a truly innocent woman without guile, without any sense of artificial propriety. He liked that about her. She was real, a part of the world he had rarely seen and never belonged to. "It isn't always so."

"The only times I have seen or felt it, it has been."

"You make it…like this."

"How?"

With a word, a sigh, a tilt of her head. With curious green eyes and soft skin and that elegant neck. With breasts and hips, soft lips…

"You talk too much." He took a step toward the bed. He should walk away. He should make certain she did not affect him any more than she already had. Eventually he would walk away, but not tonight.

"So I have been told," his bride replied, heaving a sigh that told him she'd evidently been told more than once…or twice…or hell, thirty times or more.

Blade pulled the coverlet back, exposing Lyssa's body for his eyes. Two candles lit the room with soft but sufficient light. He could see her well, and he took a moment to study. To stare. Pale and slight and seemingly fragile, she possessed a strength that was hers alone.

Another woman might shy away, reach for the covers or divert her gaze. She might use her hands to cover her breasts or the curls between her legs. Not Lyssa. Not his wife.

She deserved better than a man who planned to use her and then leave. Because whether he died in the palace, accomplishing his goal, or made a miraculous escape, he *would* leave her.

"It's all right," she said gently, as if she saw his struggle and was attempting to soothe his fears. Then she reached for him with a hand softer than any he had ever known, with a new and exciting and innocent passion. No matter what tomorrow might bring, tonight he was hers.

Blade joined her on the bed, and she rolled into him. She wanted the sensation of skin to skin, and she wanted more kisses like the one they'd shared earlier that evening. She could get lost in him so very easily.

Only last night she'd married this man just to satisfy a witch's requirement, to erase the dreams of being alone, with the thought of dismissing him when the right man came along. But what if *he* was the right man? What if *he* was the man she was destined to share her life with? It was a silly notion, given that she knew so little about him, but when he was lying beside her it seemed more than possible. It seemed quite likely. The same twists of luck that had doomed her other weddings had brought him to her in an unusual way.

Somehow, some way, she had not been the same since the moment he'd pushed inside her. He had awakened something within her body; something bright and wonderful and…needy. She had never expected to need her husband, to crave him in the pit of her stomach and even the pit of her soul.

He laid his lips on her throat and kissed her there. Lyssa closed her eyes and savored the sensations. She felt that kiss everywhere, as if he wasn't just pressed against her body but was already in it. She had never known her neck could be so sensitive, that any touch anywhere could feel so good. And then his mouth moved lower and he took a nipple into his mouth, sucking gently, rousing new and powerful sensations she had never even dreamed of. She laid her hands on his shoulders. He was so warm and hard, so different from her…no, different from everyone. Fate had led her to him, had guided her into this marriage as surely as it had led her away from the others.

While he sucked and licked, he reached between her thighs. Spread them. Stroked them. Touched her where he had last night, only this was different. Gentler and yet more powerful. She gasped and lurched, and her hips began to move in time with the motion of his fingers.

Eyes closed, she forgot where she was as she simply *felt*. The pleasure built slowly, and all too soon she knew that what she needed, what she had to have, was Blade inside her again. Though she could barely speak, she managed to whisper, "Now. Please."

Blade did not torture her; he did not make her wait. Taking his mouth from her breast—oh, she hated to see it go—he rolled on top of her and guided himself inside. It was a relief and a sharp pleasure. And it was so right.

He thrust hard, bracing himself above her. She adjusted her legs to allow him deeper access, wrapping her thighs around him, moving against and with him. As they moved, the sensations and the need grew. This was bright and wonderful. She needed him. Not just anyone. *Him.* Blade. No other man could ever make her feel this way. She was certain of it.

Each stroke was a pleasure that took her breath away; each thrust took him deeper, touched her where no other man ever had, or ever would. Nothing could feel better than this; it was impossible that her body could bear it. But it *did* feel better, again and again, until there was nothing else but *him.*

And then the pleasure peaked. It washed over her, unexpected and powerful. She cried out, clasped her body to his as a sharp release made her body quake. Blade experienced the same kind of release. She felt it, deep inside, physically and more. Deeper. His movement slowed, he dropped down atop her body.

Lyssa turned her head and found his lips with hers. The touch was soft, gentle and wonderful. In the distance, thunder rumbled. And then she said, "I would make a *terrible* nun."

He laughed. Easily, spontaneously. The sound came from deep within him. But too soon the laughter died abruptly and he rolled away from her. Away and out of the bed. She could see what he meant when he said his cock was "not always so." Now it dangled, wet and soft and very different from before. Perhaps she had been protected from the truth about relations between a man and a woman, but it didn't exactly take a genius to figure out how this worked.

"I will sleep in the main room," he said sharply.

"Why?" Had she done something wrong? Said something inappropriate? "The bed is very large, and I promise not to make demands of you in the night, if that is what you are afraid of."

He looked at her, stared at her with those magnificent eyes of his, and said, "I am not afraid."

And she knew—the same way she knew someone had been watching her from Level Two, the same way she knew Sinmora's child would be a boy, the same way she *knew* Blade was the right man for her—that he was lying.

He had not laughed in four years. He *should not* laugh now.

Blade sat on a blanket before a low fire, unable to sleep, unable to still the turmoil inside him. Lyssa was a means to an end. Nothing more. And while she was here and willing, he might as well lie with her. What man would not, when she looked at him that way? But he could not allow her to touch him inside. There was no room in his life for laughter, for gentleness or affection.

Volker had destroyed him. When the bastard had killed Runa, when he'd taken away the last of Blade's family, Volker had murdered the man Blade had once been. His sword might not have done the job, but Volker *had* killed him.

It was the guilt, more than anything else, that ate at Blade, that gnawed when he least expected it. First his mother, brutally attacked by demonic soldiers and left with child, then Runa, taken from a neighbor's home and murdered when she'd dared to scream. He had not been there to save either one of them. He should have been, he should have been there.

The embers in the hearth before him glowed, and a new flame danced. Blade stared, he did his best to forget what had just happened and focus on the past. He would have fought the soldiers who'd raped his mother if he had not been at sea. He would have killed Volker, if the ship he'd been sailing upon had docked one day earlier and he'd been at home when Runa had been taken. One day.

That had been Hagan's final voyage before retiring to Arthes and passing himself off as a respectable man instead of a pirate. It had been Blade's final voyage, too. As they had sailed toward the village his mind had been on leaving the sea and marrying a pretty girl and making a home. A home for him and for Runa. He'd had no idea what awaited him…

Blade didn't need or want that guilt to be taken away. He had no wish to be mended, and that was what it felt like when he was with Lyssa. His insides had been ripped apart, and she touched him there. She offered him more than he'd ever wanted or expected from her, and as she did, he was mended.

No more sleeping in that bed with her. No more kisses, no more laughter.

He did eventually fall asleep. And he dreamed. He didn't always dream, but when he did, he dreamed of death and blood, of Runa's disappointment that he had been too slow to save her. He should have been at home when the men came, but he had not been. He should have run faster, fought harder, and sometimes in his dreams he was fast enough. Good enough. Sleeping in front of the fire, closer to finishing his quest than he had ever been, he dreamed of water and kisses.

In his dreams Lyssa was there, and he laughed again.

Chapter Nine

"I don't understand why we have to go to the shop today," Lyssa said, trying not to sound as if she were pouting, even though she was. "A day or two to get our new home in order, to celebrate our marriage…"

"Our home is in fine order, and ours is not a real marriage, so there is nothing to celebrate," Blade said, his voice as sharp as his name. He held her hand lightly, but she knew it was not because he wanted to touch her but because he wanted her to hurry along. She tried to keep her quick steps to the higher, dryer parts of the path, avoiding the puddles left by last night's rain.

He had not looked at her, not really, all morning. Even though the beard was gone and his hair had been neatly pulled back, and the clothing he wore was respectable— though she could not say whether or not the black trousers and plain white shirt had been stolen, as the sentinel's uniform had been—he looked as rough and primitive as he had the night they'd met.

And he was walking too fast! She practically had to run to keep up with him, and running while avoiding the puddles was difficult. She was huffing and puffing, almost entirely out of breath, before she decided she'd had enough. She planted her feet on a small, almost-dry rise and came to a complete stop. The move surprised Blade. Their hands separated, and he took another step before turning around to look at her in an accusing and angry way. One would not know, from the way he stared at her, that last night they had shared incredible pleasure and he had laughed in their bed.

Lyssa crossed her arms and glared at him. "Why are you so anxious to get into the palace?"

"That's not your concern. Now come along."

Come along? Perhaps if she'd married at seventeen and had known no better, she would have allowed her husband to order her to *come along*. But she *had* not, and she *would* not. "No."

He took a short step toward her.

"And if you think you can walk into Papa's shop with me draped over your shoulder—kicking and screaming, by the way—and get him to trust you enough to work in his store and make a delivery to the palace, then you're in for a rude awakening. If you want my father to be happy, then you must make *me* happy."

Blade knew she was right. He didn't like it, but she could tell that he knew. For the first time in a long while, Lyssa felt entirely in control. She liked the feeling very much.

"What do you want?" he snapped.

"I want you to tell me why you need to get into the palace."

For a moment he hesitated. He pursed his lips, and his eyes went colder than ever before. He closed the distance between them, leaned down slightly, and lowered his voice. "The man who murdered my sister is in that palace. I intend to kill him."

In an instant she realized why Blade had left her bed last night, and her heart broke for him. His heart had been broken when he'd lost his sister, and he had given up everything to find justice for her. He did not want to find pleasure with a wife, and to laugh in bed, to share that kind of intimacy while his sister's murderer slept so close…"I'm sorry."

He did not want or accept her apology. "You didn't kill her. You have nothing to apologize for."

"Who did, then?"

"I won't tell you that," he said, and he meant it. She saw the determination in his eyes. "You'll know when it's done."

"It's not Emperor Jahn, is it?" She liked the emperor and his family, and she didn't think Blade would kill anyone other than a *very* bad man, but she had to ask.

"No."

That was a relief! "Does this man who killed your sister deserve to die?" Not a question she would have ever expected to ask of anyone, but it seemed…appropriate.

"Yes."

"Is there no other way?"

"No."

Blade did not elaborate, and she knew better than to ask him to. "And you will find a way to see it done whether I help you or not?"

"Yes."

If she didn't help him, he not only wouldn't make it into the palace, he certainly wouldn't make it out alive. Not if he was intent on murdering a palace resident. Worst of all, she suspected that he didn't care if he survived or not.

She walked to him, hooked her arm through his and looked up. "I will help you."

He started to shake his head. "I don't want your help. I simply want access."

"I *will* help you," she said again. "It's what a proper wife would do." She did not tell him that she intended to make sure he got out of the palace alive and that he stayed with her, becoming the husband neither of them had ever imagined he might be. That wasn't what he wanted to hear. Not here and now. *Not yet.*

They walked toward the shop more slowly, leaving the quiet street where they had stopped for a brief conversation and joining others on the main street. Women heading to market, sentinels hurrying toward the palace for the morning changing of the guard, children scurrying to make it to school on time. Lyssa smiled and waved at those she knew. Very few of them would have heard yet that she'd married, but soon everyone would know.

She smiled as she held Blade's arm and walked forward at a leisurely pace, even though inside she was distressed. The only reason he had married her was so he could get into the palace and take his revenge. She should not be surprised. Theirs had not been a love match; each had had their own selfish reasons for marriage. They were still all but strangers, and she had no right to expect anything of him.

If she managed to save him, if he did what he'd come here to do and lived, would he stay with her or would he leave?

This marriage had not been intended to be a permanent one. She had always planned to dissolve the union eventually, and he…She now realized that Blade had never planned to survive long enough for a dissolution ceremony to take place.

Lyssa's father was wary of his daughter's new husband being so anxious to assist in the family business, but it didn't take him long to warm up to the idea. Cyrus Tempest was getting on in years—despite Lyssa's protests that her father was *not* old—and he'd been more than happy to have his son-in-law there to unload the shipment that had arrived that afternoon, and to assist a delicate and moneyed customer with her heavy purchases. Blade was determined to make himself not only useful, but invaluable. And quickly.

Naturally the old man was suspicious of his daughter's sudden marriage, but he was more relieved than wary. Since Lyssa seemed to be happy—hell, maybe she *was* happy, for now—her father had accepted the marriage more readily than most caring fathers would have, given the unusual circumstances.

Blade was surprised that Lyssa had so easily accepted his reasoning for wishing admittance to the palace. They hadn't spoken of it since that morning, and if he had his way they would not speak of it again. Apparently as long as he wasn't intent on assassinating the emperor, she had no qualms. Then again, maybe she did and she knew better than to let him see her true intentions. Maybe she would try to stop him when the time came.

He wouldn't allow that to happen.

After a busy day they walked home together. He carried a small satchel that contained more of Lyssa's things. Dresses, combs, perhaps another nightgown. Home, for the moment, was a vine covered stone structure set back from Hagan's finer house, which was a surprisingly large house for one man and two servants. Blade wondered what Lyssa would say if she knew that their host, one of her father's best customers, had once been a pirate. Privateer, Hagan had preferred to be called, but no…pirate was a more accurate word. Blade had sailed with Hagan for a while, first as a young man excited to take to the sea, then as an older man looking for better wages than a shipbuilder's apprentice could earn. Both times he had left his family behind to make a life of his own.

If he had never gone to sea, he would have been at home to protect Runa. If he had gone home one day earlier…one day…

It was an old refrain, a way of torturing himself.

As they walked, Lyssa babbled about the day's work, the customers, the need for new inventory, *nonsense*, while Blade's eyes were on the house ahead. If he had his way, it would not be home for long. He would eventually find a way to ask Hagan to allow Lyssa to remain there after he was gone, if she desired to do so. But not yet. He didn't need the two of them putting their heads together and trying to stop him from doing what had to be done.

Before they reached the house and turned onto the path that would lead to the guest cottage, Hagan—who'd obviously been watching for their arrival—opened his front door and waved them over.

"My girl has prepared more than enough supper for three. Please, join me."

It was on the tip of Blade's tongue to refuse, but Lyssa was quicker to answer. "Lovely! I did not prepare or plan anything for supper, and Blade worked so hard today that he needs a hearty meal. Such a horrid wife I have made thus far. I must learn to be more efficient if I'm going to help my father in his shop and make a home, as well." She headed toward Hagan, and Blade reluctantly followed. As much as he dreaded small talk over a dining room table, he *was* hungry.

Besides, he was quite sure Lyssa could talk more than enough for the both of them.

Lyssa had never eaten supper at such a fine table, or had servants to bring one course after another and set it before her. A couple of days ago she had been all but prepared to move into a nunnery and now here she was, married, bedded, and eating a fine meal in a fine house. It wasn't her house, but still…she was a guest here, and she liked it.

Blade was quiet throughout the meal, but their host was gregarious and welcoming. Hagan was a bit rotund and had obviously enjoyed many meals as hearty as this one. But his cheeks were rosy, and his sparse but curly white hair was shiny and combed. He was about her father's age, she would guess, though of course it was impossible to be sure and would be rude to ask.

After a light dessert of dried fruit and a very fine cheese, Blade stood and almost abruptly said goodnight to their host. Trying her best to be a dutiful wife, one who would not dare to oppose her husband in front of others, she rose from her seat, thanked Hagan for inviting them to supper, and took Blade's arm.

They were not in love, were not a true couple, but as they walked toward their own temporary home she decided that she very much liked being a wife. Maybe it was because she had waited so long to take on that designation or maybe because she was so relieved not to be alone.

But she was a temporary wife, of that she was well aware.

There was a fire in the fireplace. Hagan again, of that she had no doubt. Not that he would have built the fire himself, but he had surely directed a servant to make the cottage ready and welcoming.

She had not suffered any unusual awkwardness all day. Work had kept her busy, and then she'd made pleasant dinner conversation with their host, but now…now she and Blade were on their own. Just the two of them. Would they come together again tonight? She could not imagine sharing a bed with her husband and not. Even now, looking at him…maybe they did not have love. Maybe they had each married for their own selfish reasons, but when she looked at him, she felt something unexpected.

He stared into the fire. Not at her. Not at all.

"I suppose I'll bathe and go to bed. It's been a very long day," she said.

Without turning to look at her, he responded with an almost distant, "Sleep well."

It was a dismissal. A curt and emotionless dismissal. Not that she expected emotion from him, but still…

"Will you join me?"

"For the bathing or the bed?" His voice was too sharp, too cold.

"Both, perhaps," she said candidly.

"I don't think either is a good idea."

"You really should look at me as you dismiss me so callously," she said, more annoyed than hurt. A man she did not love, a man who did not love her, could not hurt her. She tried to convince herself of that, but didn't quite believe it. Blade could hurt her; he was hurting her now. "I am not asking for your heart and soul, Blade. Just for your company."

At that he did turn to look at her, his eyes cold as ice and his jaw tight. "My *company*. Is that what you call it? Now that you know fuck is a vulgar word, you are reluctant to say it."

He wanted to scare her, to frighten her into scurrying away, but she could not allow that. "Call it what you will. I enjoyed sharing a bed with you. I would like to do so again, before we part ways." Many times, but she couldn't tell him that. It was probably unladylike to enjoy marital bliss so very much, not that she thought Blade cared much whether she was a lady or not.

Blade looked as if he'd eaten something bad. He didn't quite turn green, but he certainly came close. "It is not a good idea."

"Why not?"

"This is a temporary marriage, and if you were to find yourself with child…"

"Not that again." She sighed. "I wouldn't mind having a child. As a matter of fact, I very much want to have babies. Don't you want children? I thought all men wanted a son or two." She took a deep breath and gathered her courage. "Do you simply not want a child with *me*?"

The suggestion seemed to take him aback. Clearly he'd been certain he could scare her into retiring for the evening without asking so many questions.

"I'm sure when the time comes you will be an excellent, if chatty, mother," he said, his voice cold. "But raising a child alone is not easy, and I *will not* be here."

She found she was rather disturbed to hear him say the words. It had been the plan all along, of course, that their marriage be a temporary one, and she did not think that plan had changed in less than two full days. But Blade had quickly become a part of her life. Maybe because she had a part of him inside her now. Still. *Always.* And what an odd thought that was. *Always.*

"Perhaps it would be difficult, but it does happen on occasion that a woman gives birth and raises the child on her own. Husbands die, they run off with brazen women. Sometimes they just disappear." That would be the worst, she thought, to not know what had happened. "I would not be the first."

Blade looked almost stricken, for a fraction of a second, and then his expression was emotionless once again. "No. I will not allow it."

Some couples were together years before they had children, but Lyssa did not make that argument. She would not beg Blade to come to her bed. She did have a *little* pride left. "Fine. Good night," she said sharply, trying to be as cold as he had been. "I suppose you can sleep on the floor in here, since sharing a bed with me is so abhorrent to you."

He didn't tell her that she was not repulsive, nor did he indicate in any way that he regretted not sleeping with her again. As she lit a candle and walked into her bedroom, she didn't look back.

Chapter Ten

Blade tossed and turned in front of the fire. He needed to sleep while he could. As if he could get any rest with Lyssa a few feet away on the other side of the wall with an unbarred door between them.

No, there was much more than a door and a wall between them. He had to construct his own wall and keep it strong. Being with her had changed him, and he could not allow that to continue. She stole his resolve with a kiss, offered her body to him with abandon and a naive curiosity, and in doing so made him question his purpose.

If he continued to treat her as if she were a true wife, he would soon lose his passion for revenge. He could feel it fading already, a little more every time she smiled at him or even *looked* his way, and he could not let that happen. If she found herself with child he would be sucked into the role of husband and father, he would forget why he'd come to Arthes in the first place, and Volker would slip through his fingers. Worst of all...would he care? Would he allow Lyssa to steal away all that he had become? His purpose, his reason for living, was revenge. Justice. Nothing more.

Lying by the dying fire, in an almost dark room, he remembered too vividly the way he'd felt when Lyssa had wrapped her body around his. Her skin was so soft, her scent so sweet. There had been moments, wonderful, terrible moments, when he'd felt as if he could fall into her and get lost. He wanted her, and he could not have her. In the back of his mind, new thoughts teased him. Was it possible that he could kill Volker and escape with his life? That he could have his revenge *and* Lyssa?

Ridiculous. He was being led by his cock to even think that was possible.

He was finally drifting toward a restless sleep when she screamed.

His heart threatened to break through his chest as he jumped up, grabbed his dagger, and ran to her, throwing open the door to the bedroom and preparing to do battle with whoever—or whatever—had elicited that bloodcurdling scream.

No candle burned. The only light came from the remnants of the fire he had left behind. It wasn't much, but he did make out her form on the floor by the bed, huddled into a tight ball. She was trembling so hard he could see it, even though there was so little light to illuminate her. He scanned the room. The windows were tightly closed; nothing in his line of vision moved.

"What's wrong?" he snapped.

Lyssa lifted her head. "Is she still here? The woman who tried to kill me…where is she? Where did she go?"

Blade saw no one, but there were many dark shadows someone might hide within. He lit a candle and held it high as he searched the small room. There was no sign of an intruder and no indication that anyone had been here moments earlier, when Lyssa had screamed.

"A dream," he said, relaxing. "It was just a dream."

"It was not a dream!" Lyssa insisted. "I felt her hands on my throat, and she said…she said I had to die. She said I had to die before I ruined everything."

She looked at him then, and after a short pause she gave him a small, weak smile.

"What?" he snapped.

"I have never seen a naked man wielding a dagger before. Please be careful with those sharp edges, husband."

He had a candle in one hand and his dagger in the other. He'd been so alarmed by her scream he'd given no thought to his state of undress until she'd pointed it out to him.

"I told you, I sleep naked," he said simply.

"Yes, I am aware." With that, Lyssa rose to her feet. She remained unsteady. In spite of her teasing she was still unsettled by fear.

"I have had dreams that seemed real," he said, trying to soothe her in the only way he knew how. With reason.

"It didn't feel like a dream at all." Lyssa gave into her wobbly knees and sat on the side of the bed, raising her hand to her throat. "I swear, my neck actually hurts."

Blade stepped toward her. He dismissed his state of undress from his mind. She'd seen him this way before, and he would not pretend to be modest now. "There's no one here, it had to be…" He stopped in mid-sentence, staring down at this woman who was his wife. He lowered the candle slightly, for the light. Just to be sure.

On the side of her lovely throat was a red mark that looked as if it might turn into a bruise by morning. A long, slender red mark, as if a finger had squeezed there.

He spun around to search the room again, wondering if he'd missed something. Or some*one*. Lyssa repeated his soothing words. "Just a dream." And then she sighed. "Dear me. The view is just as enchanting from the rear as it was from the front, husband."

Over the next few days Lyssa and Blade fell into a stale, frustrating rhythm. By day they both worked in the store with her father. Sinmora had once been a great help there, but she'd been ill several days this week and had stayed home. It was the baby making her ill, Lyssa reasoned. The baby her father and stepmother had not yet told her about. The son he had always wanted.

Supper was sometimes shared with Hagan Elmar and sometimes eaten in the guest cottage, which was beginning to feel like home to her. Blade was never inclined to indulge in conversation, whether there were three for dinner or only two. And after dinner...after dinner Blade Renshaw did his best not to even glance in her direction. He showed no interest in sharing a bed with her. Had she done something wrong? Did he dislike her so intensely?

She was disappointed, but she would not beg for her husband's attentions. She'd survived the humiliation of four failed weddings, and she would survive this. At least no one but the two of them knew the truth of their situation. Her humiliation was a private one. Was she Bad Luck Lyssa still? Apparently so. Terrible Tempest? No, now she was Wretched Renshaw.

Blade put on a good show for her father, playing the devoted husband. He even went to church with her on the seventh day. Some Columbyanans believed in the One God, while others worshipped many. Lyssa knew that most sailors prayed to many gods—gods of the sea, the sky, the thunder—and Blade had once been a sailor. Still, while sitting in church, he'd seemed to listen to the priest. He did not squirm or doze off, as her Papa often did. But if he appeared to be a dutiful husband, she knew it was only so he could gain access to the palace. When they were alone, she might as well have been a stranger.

At least there had been no more dreams that felt to be more than dreams. No more waking feeling as if there were hands around her throat, no more sensation of the air being sucked from her lungs. That dream had been very much like the others, those old dreams of being alone in a cold, stone room. They were more real than any dream should be, with smell and touch and sound so true...how could they be mere dreams?

The day Blade had been waiting for finally arrived. There was a delivery to be made to the palace: specially ordered fabrics for the empress; sweets for the princes and princesses; spices for the imperial kitchen. As it looked as if Blade would one day be taking over the business, she mentioned to her father that it would be wise to acquaint him with their best customer. She felt guilty, keeping Blade's secret from her father. He was not a true husband to her, and he had no intention of becoming a shopkeeper. If he had his way he would die exacting his revenge.

Of course, her father had his own secrets. He still hadn't shared his news about the baby Sinmora carried. What else had he kept from her? Blade certainly had secrets, secrets he hid well. If the two men in her life were so skilled at deception, how could she trust...anyone? Perhaps she had been hopelessly naive all her life, believing that everyone around her was exactly as they appeared to be.

On this lovely, slightly cool afternoon, the three of them—Lyssa, her father, and her husband—walked toward the palace, each of them carrying goods to be delivered. Her heart beat too fast; her mouth was dry. Just because they were going into the palace, as Blade wanted, that didn't mean he would get his revenge today. The palace was large, with multiple levels. Ten above ground and at least two below. On those levels there were many rooms, hallways, and people. There were even, she had heard, secret rooms and passages. He might not find the person he sought today. She so wished he would not!

The palace was in view, the sentinels guarding the entrance mere feet ahead, when Lyssa stumbled and then stuttered to a halt. As she had days earlier, she lifted her head and looked up at a window on Level Two. No one stood there, there was no sign that anyone occupied that room, but she knew—she *knew*—that the woman who had tried to strangle her was there. Watching. Waiting.

No, not a woman. A *demon*. Whispered words filled her head. *Witch. Death. Ksana. Darkness. Alone.* Every nightmare, every fear, was expressed in those few words that assaulted her. And Ksana…she had heard of those demon daughters called Ksana, but she'd never believed them to be real. They were said to be the worst of the lot; demon daughters whose mothers died in childbirth, unable to withstand the poisonous nature of their babies, demon daughters who could kill with a kiss. All beautiful, all deadly…She had thought the Ksanas to be myth, or at the very least an exaggeration. But no, they were real. She knew that now. And one was speaking to her now in a way she had never known possible.

Alone, alone, alone…

Lyssa became aware that both her husband and her father were calling her name. She did not know how many times they'd called to her, but they both looked concerned. Blade's concern had to be an act. He did not care for her or about her. He would not care if she dropped dead here in the street, mysteriously killed by some dark magic, so long as he got into the palace first.

Darkness and light, the witch Vellance had said. Was this what she'd been talking about so long ago?

"I can't go in there," Lyssa said, handing the sack of spices to her father.

"Why not?" Blade asked.

"Are you ill?" Her Papa leaned in close, looking into her eyes. He was truly concerned.

"I…I…" Would they believe her if she told them she was certain that if she stepped into that palace she would never leave? Would they believe her if she said there was a demon on Level Two, a Ksana demon determined to see her dead? She could already see the answer in Blade's expression. He thought she was stalling to keep him from his goal.

Maybe she was. Not consciously, of course, but…she wasn't ready to lose him. She would never be ready to lose him! If he managed to kill the man he sought and was lucky enough to escape, he would no longer need her. If he died, as he was certainly prepared to do, then she would be a widow. And alone, so horribly, completely alone.

"Dear, you're much too pale," her father said. He took the fabric from Blade and dismissed them both, as he headed for the palace entrance. "Blade, take her back to the shop and relieve Sinmora. She hasn't been feeling well, either, and I'm sure she'll be glad to return home earlier than expected." He glanced back over his shoulder and smiled. "Perhaps the two women in my life are suffering from a similar malady."

Blade glared at her. "I'm sure Lyssa can return to the shop on her own. She does not need my help, and I would like to meet the palace purchasing agent if I'm to be fully involved in the business."

"Another time," Cyrus called without even glancing back. "Lyssa appears to be much too wobbly to proceed on her own." A moment later he was gone, walking past the sentinels who knew him well, and soon disappearing from view.

They did not immediately retreat. Lyssa's fear faded, but it did not disappear. Life continued all around them, residents of the city walking past and around.

"Why?" Blade finally whispered.

"I did not stop you on purpose," Lyssa said. "I really do feel…ill."

He glared at her. The tension in his body was so high she did not dare to move any closer. At this moment he was more of a danger to her than any demon child. She stood firmly between him and his goal. Even though she had assisted him to this point, she was an obstacle.

Blade not only expected to die, he wanted death. He craved it.

Taking a deep breath, she closed her eyes. Since her birthday—since her marriage—everything had changed. She knew things she should not. She felt danger where before there had been none. In truth, her world was spinning out of control.

"You will have another chance." She reached out and grabbed his arm because she needed the support. He did not shake away her touch, as she'd thought he might. He was so angry. Angry with her, frustrated because he was so near to his goal but not near enough.

Her father was inside the palace. The feeling of evil watching from above had faded, and still Lyssa reeled. It was like she was caught in a waking dream. While life went on around her, solid and real, she saw a sword, the blade flashing as it had once done in a nightmare. She saw her husband holding that sword, and she saw the man he had come here to kill. It was real and not real, truth and fantasy. Her knees threatened to buckle, but she remained strong. What choice did she have?

She took a step closer, tilted her head back and looked into Blade's angry eyes. "You will kill him, this man who murdered your sister. But not today, Blade. The time is not right."

One of the words the demon had whispered was *witch*. Was that what she had become? Whatever she was, whatever she'd become, she knew Blade would get his revenge. Soon. For a vengeance born out of love for his sister, he would risk his life. She didn't see what would happen after that—if he would die, or if he would survive and leave her. Either way, he had no intention of being the husband she needed and wanted.

She loved him. Unexpectedly, strongly, undeniably. And she was suddenly heartbroken that he would never return that love.

Chapter Eleven

Lyssa was not herself, and hadn't been from the moment she'd stumbled outside the palace—so close to Volker, so damn close and still…not nearly close enough. After an afternoon spent minding the shop, he escorted her into the home they shared. She was subdued; she did not smile; she did not once look at him as if she thought she could fix his life. Fix *him*, more rightly.

She'd even declined Hagan's invitation to supper before Blade could do it himself. She liked Hagan; she enjoyed dining with him, chatting over a meal someone else had prepared. But tonight…Tonight she was shaken and clearly not in the mood for company.

Once inside the cottage, she'd sliced bread and cheese and fruit, and eaten without talking. It wasn't like her not to carry on a one-sided conversation while they walked or ate or worked. He should be glad. He'd never been fond of chattering women. But sitting at the small table, fire blazing, candles lit, he missed the sound of Lyssa's voice. In a perverse way he craved it.

Finally he was compelled to ask, "What's wrong. Are you truly ill?"

"Not ill," she said, tearing off a piece of bread and playing with it. "But…"

"But what?" He didn't mean to snap, but he did.

She lifted her head and looked at him squarely for the first time in hours. Those green eyes were so bright and clear and innocent. If he were another man, he could fall into her and get lost. Losing himself in a woman wasn't an option in this life he'd chosen.

"Something is wrong with me," she said. "Ever since…ever since we were married, I've been different. I know things I should not, I have dreams that are more than dreams, and…and…" She stopped, staring down into her lap as if she could not bear to look at him any longer.

"Dammit, Lyssa, spit it out!"

She hesitated, but not for long. "Last week I delivered some goods to an old woman who does not get around very well." Still she did not look at him. "I touched her bad knee, and she said it felt instantly better. And this evening as we were walking home I saw her walking down the street. Quite spryly, I might add."

"That doesn't mean…"

She lifted her head and stared at him, and he wished she'd continued to look away. Lyssa, his happy wife, this naive and innocent person who lived in a world so unlike his own, was tortured. "There's more. This afternoon, while I was standing mere feet from the palace entrance, I told you that you would kill the man who murdered your sister. But I didn't tell you everything." She took a deep breath, exhaled slowly. "I actually saw you killing a man. I saw it in my head as clear as day, as clearly as if it were happening right before my eyes. He had a beard and brown eyes, and wore a very nice cloak. I recognized him, I've seen him in the palace, but I do not know his name. He was surprised when you killed him with your sword. It was so real. I smelled the blood, I watched his eyes go vacant…."

"I don't have a sword," Blade said. A beard, brown eyes, a nice cloak…maybe she'd seen Volker before and pulled that description out of her head. Or else she was guessing. Many men had beards and brown eyes.

"You will obtain one before you do what you came here to do."

She sounded so confident, so sure of herself. "Is that why you're upset, because you imagined me killing…this man?" He almost slipped and used Volker's name, but caught himself in time.

Her eyes shone more brightly. "No. I imagined nothing. I *saw*. I *heard*. And I've seen more than what you've come here to do, much more." Her fingers flexed, her throat worked as she swallowed nervously. "There is a demon daughter in that palace, Blade. A Ksana. And she wants…she intends to kill you. You, me…one or both of us. I just can't see that part clearly. But she said I would be alone, she whispered it in my ear, in my head. Such a horrible word, alone. I am tired of hearing it, again and again."

"Why didn't you mention this earlier?" After all, they had spent hours together, in the shop. Customers had come and gone, true, but there had been more than one opportunity for her to tell this tale. She had not.

"I did. I told you that you would kill this man just…not today." She looked down. "I wanted to think on the details before I said any more. It's all just so wrong, in so many ways."

The stress of this "marriage" was obviously too much for Lyssa. She was losing her mind, or else she was lying to him, trying to scare him away, trying to make him change his mind. Nothing and no one would keep him from killing Miron Volker, and if that was her game she was wasting her breath.

"The only way this could be happening, the only way you could know things like this is if you're a witch. You're not a witch, are you?" He tried to make his voice light, as if he were teasing her. He expected a quick "No!" but Lyssa said nothing.

A witch. A witch like the old hag who had warned her that she had to be a bedded wife before she turned twenty-three. She'd suspected as much this afternoon, standing before the palace with a demon whispering in her ear, and again moments later, with visions of a bearded man's death playing in her head as clearly as if it were happening before her at that moment. But when the words had come out of Blade's mouth it had become all too real.

Lyssa did not remember her mother. Her father had told her stories; sweet, normal stories of a wonderful woman who had died too soon. But she now knew that her father could lie when it suited him. He had withheld the news about the baby Sinmora carried, and keeping that secret was almost as egregious as a lie. He could, and did, withhold information.

Had her mother been a witch? Thanks to that shared blood, did she herself possess dark powers that slept within her?

No, they did not sleep. Not anymore. Blade had awakened the witch in her the night they'd been married, the night he'd taken her against a stone wall. Without love or tenderness, without any reason on her part other than her fear of living her life alone.

If she had not gone to the tavern, if she'd accepted her fate and become a nun or an old maid, would the witch in her have been awakened? She suspected—no, she *knew*— not.

There was no going back, no undoing what had been done. She'd made her choice and these were the consequences.

She so wished that there was someone she trusted to teach her, to answer her questions. What she saw, were they true visions of what was to be or only what might be? Blade wanted his sister's murderer dead; the Ksana demon wanted Lyssa and her new husband dead. One or both. And honestly, she could not be *alone* if she was dead. She did wish the demon would pick a threat and stick with it.

Surely a true witch would not be so confused.

Again Blade left Lyssa on her own in the bedroom. He would sleep on the floor by the fire, keeping his distance, leaving her alone when the very reason for their marriage was so she would *not* be alone.

Had she made a mistake by marrying him? Even knowing what she now knew, she didn't think so. No. He'd been the only suitable answer to an immediate dilemma, a solution to a problem which would have soon sent her to a nunnery. He was supposed to be temporary, a man to meet certain requirements only until the right man came along. She'd been so clever, so sure of herself. She had never expected to discover that she had romantic notions about her husband.

Notions he obviously did not share.

She donned her nightdress and crawled beneath the covers. A nice, big, soft bed should be a luxury, but she was accustomed to a narrower, harder one. This bed seemed much too large for one person alone. There was room for Blade here. More than enough room.

She rolled over and blew out the single candle that burned on her bedside table, then flopped onto her back, sighed in dismay at finding herself alone once more and shut her eyes, as if that simple act alone would force her to sleep.

She lay there for a few long moments, eyes closed, heart beating too hard, attempting to will herself to sleep. Maybe she and Blade were both wrong. Maybe by morning she would have a reasonable explanation for what she'd experienced today. Illness, perhaps, or a temporary breakdown of some kind. Maybe the dried meat she'd eaten at midday had been bad. She took deep, even breaths and thought of pleasant things. Flowers and butterflies and sweet cake. It wasn't easy to leave the events of the day behind and claim blessed sleep, but she was almost there when she heard it.

Breathing. Not hers, and not Blade's. Not only would she have heard him open the bedroom door if he'd entered, that was not his breath. It was lighter, faster....She opened her eyes, wondering if she'd fallen asleep and was only dreaming that she had insomnia.

Above her, looking down, floating no more than a foot above her face, flaming red eyes shone bright in the darkness.

Lyssa rolled off the bed, making her escape. Her feet hit the floor, and she sprinted toward the door. Well, she sprinted to the place where she thought the door should be and met a solid wall. The room was entirely dark, and she was more than a little disoriented.

A young woman's sweet and confident voice whispered, "Don't go, Lyssa. We have so much to talk about before you die. You, or him, or both. If he is dead you are no threat to us, no threat at all. If you are dead, he is just another man." It was the same voice that had whispered to her outside the palace.

Lyssa felt for the wall and made her way along it to where the door handle should be. Nothing. Frantically, her hands skimming the wall, she searched for it until she finally noted—a good two feet to her right—a sliver of light peeking through a crevice. With that as a guide she reached again for the handle and found it. She threw the door open on a soft titter of laughter.

As she ran into the room, Blade sat up sharply, then stood in a smooth, graceful motion. And damned if he wasn't naked again.

"What's wrong?" Behind him the last of the fire burned gently. She could not see his face—or anything else—with the light behind him, but she was heartened just to be in the same room with him.

"Eyes," she said, knowing as she spoke that her single word made no sense. "Red eyes, like fire. She laughed, and she said…she said…" She couldn't repeat the words, didn't even want to think of them.

"She?"

"That demon who lives on Level Two of the palace."

He relaxed. She saw it in the shift of his shoulders, heard it in his voice as he said, "It was just a dream, Lyssa."

She walked toward him. "I can't be alone. I can't sleep in that room without you in the bed beside me. I won't…I won't ask for anything else, but please, Blade." She was close now, just a couple of feet away. "I am stronger with you than I am without you. And I know you don't want to hear it, but…you're stronger with me, too. Separately we're a scared girl who jumps at shadows and a man willing to die for revenge. Together we're…"

"Together we're what?" Blade snapped.

"More," Lyssa said, and as the word left her mouth she knew to her very soul that it was true.

♦ ♦ ♦

Princess stood at the window and smiled into the night. She was here, in her room in the palace, and she was also there. The worry that such a pathetic creature could threaten her and her kind was ridiculous. The Ksanas' shared fear of the witch and the blade, the knowing from the universe that had come to each of them as their gifts manifested and grew, could not be correct. Lyssa Tempest was not a monster who could ruin a promising future, she was a mouse. Just to be safe, Princess would make sure she would soon be a dead mouse, but she was not afraid. Not of a witch, not of anyone.

Lyssa's magic made it possible for a connection to be made from a distance. Princess had attempted to reach for the husband as well, to slip into his head, his thoughts, but he was kept from her. Physical distance and his lack of magic protected him, in this one matter. Nothing would protect him from death, when the time came.

She was hungry now. Appearing in Lyssa's room had drained her, just as attempting to strangle the girl several nights before had. When she did not use her powers she could go for weeks, months even, without feeding.

If Father expected to see this done, he had better provide her with the appropriate nourishment.

Her sisters were sleeping as she silently walked to the door. She knocked once. Someone was always just outside the door. She hated being locked in, but she knew it wouldn't last. She and her sisters—and there were many more sisters than the two who shared this room with her—would soon be free. And no one would be able to stop them.

A guard opened the door. He was loyal to Father, but did not know the reason for his current duty. He had not been warned, or else he had not been well informed. If he had, he would never have opened the door. Father fed her drunks and wanderers, and other men who would not be missed, but as Princess looked at the guard, she was taken by his strength and his beauty. He would feed her well.

She smiled. Her smile was irresistible, she knew. "I cannot sleep," she whispered, "and I don't want to disturb the others. Can I step into the hall and talk to you for a while? I'm so lonely."

Princess knew what the guard saw. A small, young female, pretty to a fault, too overtly sensuous for her age. When she caught his eyes with hers she knew he was lost. In her blue eyes he saw no threat. None at all.

"Of course," he said, and he opened the door wider for her. He glanced behind her and saw that she'd been telling the truth. Her sisters were asleep.

Princess stepped into the hallway, glancing to her right and then to her left. No one else was wandering the hallways on this level of the palace at the moment, though there were more demons in rooms off other hallways. They were close by, imprisoned as she had been imprisoned. But she wasn't imprisoned now. She was free. *Almost* free.

It occurred to her that she could run after she fed. Down the hall, down the stairs, into the night. No one would stop her, and it would be morning before anyone realized she had gone. But then what? Her opportunities for power were here, in her Father's hands. It would be foolish to escape now.

"Why can't you sleep?" the guard asked, once the door was gently closed behind her. They were alone in the long hallway. "Did you have a bad dream?"

"I did," she said. "I dreamed that there were fiery red eyes floating above my head, and the person behind those eyes wanted me dead."

"That *is* scary," he admitted. "But it was just a dream."

"Was it?" She took a step closer to him. "Can you be sure? There's magic all around us. Some of that magic is dark. What if..." She batted her lashes. "What if some dark witch is trying to kill me?"

The guard laid a hand on her shoulder, an offered comfort. "Minister Volker has gone to great lengths to protect you and your sisters from those who would do you harm, though I am not of a high enough rank to be told the details of your situation. But I am here to protect you, and you have nothing to fear."

"I suppose that's true," she said, and then she laid her head on his chest and sighed. For a moment the sentinel held his breath. He was confused, conflicted. And he wanted her, even though he knew he should not.

For a moment Princess wondered if she would ever be able to lie with a man. A kiss was all it took to empty a man of his essence, but if she took him into her body, if she were to lie beneath him...perhaps, one day, but she suspected she would never know that particular pleasure. Her body was poison inside. Perhaps she would be forever a virgin. A virginal demon; a woman and not a woman.

"My lady, you should not..." The sentinel choked on his words.

Princess lifted her head and looked up at him. He saw a vulnerable, confused, desirable girl. She saw beauty and power and nourishment. "Would you kiss me? I feel so alone here, so lost."

"I should not," he protested without conviction.

"Just a kiss. A kiss will make me feel so much better." Princess looked him in the eye and captured him. The guard was physically superior, but his mind was malleable. And he was already hers.

Her lips met his, and for a moment—a very short moment—it was nothing more than a kiss. It was pleasurable, stirring. And then it began. She felt his essence pouring into her, filling her mouth and her throat and then her entire being. He felt it, too, but he was powerless to move away. The strength was all hers now. She had the power; she was in control. Her tongue thrust into his mouth as she attempted to lick away all he had.

Princess closed her eyes because she did not wish to see such a handsome man waste away to nothing. She didn't want to watch him shrivel and shrink. There was nothing to be done for what she felt of his decline, but she did not wish to see. Soon they sank—together—to the floor, as he could no longer stand. His lips were dry, and he no longer fought. He did not have the strength to fight. When the last of his life force left his body she broke the connection, opened her eyes, and watched him turn to dust and bones.

She stood, and with her hands brushed away the dust that clung to her nightgown. She felt so much better, so much stronger! It was a shame the sentinel had to die, but there was nothing to be done for it. His sacrifice would serve them all well.

She suspected that before Lyssa Tempest and her man died, many more sentinels would be called upon to make the same sacrifice. It would take a lot of power to do what had to be done.

Blade turned away from Lyssa. He had not been able to talk her into returning to bed unaccompanied. When he'd tried to order her to bed she'd stubbornly lain down on the floor beside him and refused to move. When he'd scooted away, she'd scooted with him. When he sat up, she sat up, too, and leaned into him. He'd finally decided that if she was going to insist on sleeping with him, they might as well do it in a bed. He *could* resist her. He *could* sleep with her without indulging in a husband's pleasure.

Resisting her wouldn't be easy, but…

It didn't help when they settled down into the bed and she pressed her chest against his back, wrapping an arm around him, fitting her body to his. If he hadn't felt her body trembling he would have shaken her off, but doing so would be a waste of time, he convinced himself. She would follow; she would not let go. She was truly scared.

So was he. The words she'd spoken with so much fear and confidence scared him to his bones. *Together we are more.*

He didn't want to be more, didn't *need* to be more. His life was simple; his *goal* was simple. The end was in sight, and he could not allow Lyssa to distract him from it.

"I don't understand why you felt the need to put on pants before coming to bed," she whispered. "You would be more comfortable naked, I'm sure, since that is how you usually sleep."

"It seemed like the thing to do."

She apparently could not let the matter go. Did she ever let anything go? From his limited experience, he would have to say no.

"I have seen you naked several times, and we have fucked more than once, so—"

"Lyssa!"

"I know it is a vulgar word, but you have heard me say it before, so I don't understand why I should demur now."

"Go to sleep," he said gruffly.

She sighed. "I will try, but it won't be easy."

Easy? Was anything to do with Lyssa ever *easy*?

She didn't drift off to sleep, and neither did he. She squirmed, moved about as if trying to get comfortable while holding onto him. Every motion, no matter how small, brought her closer, rubbed her skin again his, made him want her more. Perhaps if he slept she would follow, but his mind was spinning. Tension shot through his entire body, until he felt as if his nerves were on fire. Sleep was not coming. At the moment he felt as if he would never sleep again.

He should not have married her. He should have ignored her cries for help and let Gnarly Red have her. She would be another man's problem then.

No. The idea of any man hurting her made his chest tight. The thought of another man having her in his bed was…impossible. But he could have—and should have —refused her marriage proposal and escorted her home. She was not a part of his plan; he could not afford to care about her. He couldn't even afford to like her, not if she was going to get in the way of a plan four years in the making.

After a while she whispered, her breath warm against his back, her lips *right there*, "How did you get the scar on your chest?"

"It doesn't matter. Go to sleep."

"I can't. I feel like a clock that's been too tightly wound."

Blade groaned. As if it wasn't bad enough that he was hard more often than not these days. As if he didn't throb when she told him what she wanted—directly or not so directly. He knew how to unwind her clock, but every time he was inside her he felt himself shift a little bit. Lyssa said she was changing, and though he could never tell her so, she was not alone. She made him question everything…and that was a risk he could not take. He had to remain focused on revenge. No, not revenge, justice. Justice for Runa, at any cost.

More. He could not afford to be more than he was. Could not afford to push his plans back. His hate faded when he was with Lyssa, when she smiled at him, when she chattered on about nothing. Life threatened to become *more*.

She squirmed, shifted, pressed her body against his while her arm encircled him and her gentle hand brushed against his bare chest. Since she'd asked about the scar Volker had given him, she apparently wanted to touch it. Caress it with the soft tips of her fingers.

Finally he rolled over, threw her onto her back and glared down at her. He could barely see her face, but he knew exactly what she would look like at this moment. Hopeful, lips parted, green eyes dancing. So pretty and soft and…kind.

He could not be kind to her in return. If kindness was what she wanted, she should have married someone else. "I know how to make you be still." He threw the coverlet to the end of the bed and with rough hands pulled the hem of her nightdress up. She assisted, lifting her hips, wiggling to position herself and open her thighs. She thought he was going to give her exactly what she wanted, but she was wrong.

"There's more than one way to ease your suffering, wife," he said as he placed one hand between her legs.

"I didn't say I was suff—oh!" Her hips lurched as he found the nub at her entrance and circled his thumb there.

"Don't talk, just lie there and feel."

"It does feel…" She didn't finish the sentence. Didn't need to. Her hips moved in a gentle rhythm against his hand, and her breathing changed. She sighed and moaned and made small, maddening noises deep in her throat. Had she really been a virgin a week ago? Was she really, truly his wife?

No, he could not let his mind go there, could not pretend that this marriage was real. The rhythm of her hips grew faster, harder. He thrust two fingers inside her and she crested, huskily calling his name as her body spasmed. And then she drifted into the mattress with a satisfied sigh.

"That was…lovely, and very unexpected, I must say. But…but what about you?"

Blade removed his hand from her before saying, as coldly as possible, "I don't want you."

Another woman would have cried or kicked him out of the bed. Another woman would have railed at him for being so cruel. But Lyssa didn't hesitate. She simply reached out and placed a hand on his painfully hard length as she whispered, "Liar."

He turned his back to her, ignoring his wife once more. Or trying to. She snuggled against his back again and even placed a gentle kiss on his spine. And right before she fell asleep she whispered once more, *"Such a liar."*

Hagan was an early riser, Blade knew, so he didn't hesitate to knock on the man's door just after the sun rose. Lyssa was preparing breakfast. He didn't have much time, but he did need a word with Hagan. Alone.

The older man admitted Blade into the house himself, as he often did. Wearing a bright red dressing gown, his hair uncombed, Hagan was not prepared for visitors but he was wide awake. In the dining room, he offered Blade tea. Blade declined, as they both sat at the table.

They were alone, no Lyssa or servants present, so Blade spoke plainly.

"It was Miron Volker who killed Runa."

Hagan's hands shook and he set his teacup down too hard. He was obviously unprepared for such a conversation. *"Minister* Volker?"

"Yes."

"Are you…sure?"

"Of course I'm sure! I saw him kill her, and I looked him in the eye when he tried to kill me. I didn't know his name, then, but now I do."

Hagan shook his head. "You can't possibly think to get away with…"

"No," Blade said in a lowered voice. "I won't get away with it. I won't escape."

"There has to be another way…"

"There is not."

Hagan's cook, a youngish woman with wild red hair, walked into the dining room carrying a tray of sweet rolls and jam. When she saw Blade she started a bit, surprised to see such an early visitor, then she placed the tray on the able and said, "I'll be right back with another plate and more rolls. Eggs will be ready shortly."

"I won't be eating," Blade said.

Hagan waved the cook away with an impatient hand, and she went.

"You have a wife, now," Hagan whispered. "You cannot throw your life away!"

Blade did not argue that Lyssa was not a true wife. He could not even say that he didn't care. He whispered, too, in case the cook had her ear pressed to the other side of the dining room door. "When I die, will you let her stay here? She will need a home." She would need a friend even more than a cozy cottage, he suspected.

"Of course she can stay, but there is no need. Together we can find another way to see this done."

If there was another way, he would have thought of it already. "No. There is no other way."

"Emperor Jahn…"

"Will not hang one of his own ministers for killing one of the Isen Demon's daughters," Blade finished, his voice sharp.

Hagan paled. "The timing of Runa's birth…I cannot say I never wondered. I did hope I was wrong. I'm so sorry."

No one else would care. No one else would see that Volker was punished. "Lyssa." Blade said simply. "Take care of her."

Hagan nodded, once. It was enough.

Blade had thought about leaving her, Lyssa knew. Even when he'd shown her pleasure and denied himself, he had thought of simply walking away. He said nothing to that effect; his actions and words when others were present had not changed. To her friends and family, he appeared to be a loving husband. All of her friends and more than a few acquaintances had stopped by the shop to meet him, and she could tell that they were envious. After all, Blade was handsome and attentive, a dream husband—at least outwardly. He was the man who had broken the curse, who had survived marriage to Terrible Tempest. He did not show his intentions to the world, but Lyssa knew that for a while now he had considered leaving her without offering a word of explanation.

But he *hadn't* left. She scared him—she knew that, too—but she didn't scare him enough to give up his goal.

Blade thought death was all he had to offer the world, that once he had avenged his sister his life would be over. Pointless. Worthless. Without meaning. He was wrong. Unfortunately, he did not believe her.

Her husband was a hard worker and a determined man; to all eyes the man she had been waiting for all these years. She knew what others did not; that he had settled into the job with her father only to patiently wait for another opportunity to access the palace. She spent every frustrating day trying to think of a way to stop him.

Edine, who had been a wife for three years now, had offered to show Lyssa how to prepare a few of her husband's favorite foods. That devoted husband's mother was currently watching the children for a few hours so Edine could spend some time with her oldest friend. Lyssa had worried a bit about leaving Blade and her father alone at the store, but business was slow this late in the afternoon, and besides…the two men got along very well. That would not be the case if Cyrus Tempest knew the truth about his son-in-law, but as he did not, all would be well. For a while.

Lyssa had seen Edine several times since her marriage to Blade, but they had not been on their own. There were always children or a husband or a father around. With the window opened and the doors closed, they were on their own now in the cottage Edine shared with her husband and two young children. Edine wasted no time. She smiled widely and asked, "How do you like being married?"

"It's very nice." Lyssa twisted her hands just a little, flexed her fingers and shifted her feet. She hated to lie, especially to a friend, and here she was, trapped in an enormous lie! But being married *was* very nice. That much was the truth.

Edine's smile faded. "Nice? Blade is so handsome, and strong. Surely you can come up with a word better than *nice* to describe him. Is he an attentive husband? A good kisser? How is he in bed?"

"Oh, you want to know about the fucking."

Edine actually drew back a bit. "Lyssa Tempest! I mean, Lyssa Renshaw! Such language."

"I know it is a vulgar word, but…"

"*Very* vulgar."

"Well, what do *you* call it?"

"Sinmora didn't prepare you for marriage at all," Edine said in a disapproving tone. "You cannot cook, and you don't even know that what you said is entirely unacceptable for a lady."

"I'm not a lady. I'm a shopkeeper's daughter and a shopkeeper's wife." *And perhaps a witch*, though she kept that thought to herself. "Sinmora said it was a husband's place to instruct a wife. She never did go into details about what that instruction might include. Or what it might be called."

"Yin will, on occasion, call it a poke. A word I detest, by the way."

"I can understand why." Lyssa wrinkled her nose.

"He thinks it's roguish and charming, but he's mistaken." Edine lifted her eyebrows in an expression that spoke of loving exasperation. "My mother calls it my wifely duty, which doesn't seem any better than a poke. It has never felt much like a duty to me," she added in a lowered voice.

Nor to me. "Well, if I can't say…that word, what should I call it?"

Edine smiled. "I like to call it making love."

Making love. She liked that, though it wasn't entirely accurate where she and Blade were concerned. He didn't love her. "Many people who are not in love share their bodies."

"Then it's a poke, or what you said, but when a man and woman are truly in love, the act is simply not the same."

Lyssa wondered if she occasionally thought herself in love with Blade simply because he made her feel good, on those few occasions when they'd…well, call it what you would, he had been inside her in more ways than one. But when she tried to imagine any other man in her bed—in her body—she could not. Would not.

Making love.

Lyssa found she was anxious to change the subject. How could she explain to her friend that Blade had come into her life as a temporary solution and now he didn't feel temporary at all? Love had never been a part of the plan, so why did the words "making love" feel so right? Yes, best to avoid that particular subject.

"If you don't teach me how to cook, I will be a poor wife indeed."

That was all it took to get Edine started. A pie, stew and a quick bread. Lyssa watched, trying to absorb it all. She and Edine talked the entire time, their conversations flitting back and forth between culinary pursuits, children, parents, the weather and new shoes and husbands, with barely a breath between subjects. Perhaps their constant conversation was the reason Edine's hand slipped and she cut the palm of her other hand, a deep cut from which blood began pouring.

Edine dropped the knife and stepped away from the table, staring at the sliced flesh and the blood that filled her palm. "Damnation!" Without lifting her head to look at Lyssa, Edine lifted her uninjured hand and pointed to the hearth. "There's a basket of bandages and ointments next to the small pot."

Instead of fetching the basket, Lyssa reached out and grabbed her friend's hand. "How bad is it?"

"Bad enough. It stings like the devil! And look at all the blood." Edine grimaced as she grabbed a linen towel and placed it under her hand so blood wouldn't drip on her floor.

Acting on instinct, Lyssa took Edine's hand in her own. The already bloodied linen dropped to the floor. The cut was deep, the gash too severe to be mended by ointment and a strip of linen. Lyssa's mind momentarily turned to doctors and stitches and weeks of immobility.

And there it was again, that green fog that floated above the wound, an unnatural glow much like the one she'd noted above Madam Azar's knee. Without thinking, Lyssa laid her other hand over Edine's and tightly enveloped her friend's damaged hand.

Lyssa's body twitched a bit. A glimmer of green light slipped from between her fingers. Cold fire, just like before, along with a sensation of…power. Edine jumped, and she tried to pull her hand away, but Lyssa held on tight. Just a few seconds, that was all the time she needed. As soon as the light died Edine jerked her hand away. She stepped back, wiped away the blood from one hand with the other, and—pale as milk—she held up her hand, palm facing Lyssa.

The blood remained, but the cut was gone.

"How did you do that?" Edine whispered.

Lyssa licked her lips. If she had known an appropriate curse word, she would have used it. The only word that came to her was no. *No, no, no, no.* She wanted to deny that which was right before her eyes, she wanted to run and hide.

"The damage was probably not as bad as we thought…." she said, her voice weak, unconvincing even to her own ears.

"Even if it was just a scratch, it shouldn't be *gone.*" Eyes widening, Edine moved back, and around, putting the table between her and Lyssa. "You're a witch—or a demon."

Lyssa thought about denying the charge, but how? She had done what she had done. For weeks she'd tried her best to ignore all the signs, to dismiss what she saw and felt and experienced. She could not ignore this, much as she would like to.

"Just because I happen to have some magical abilities, that doesn't make me a demon. And…there are some good witches, you know."

Edine shook her head. She looked at the floor, at her hand, at the food on the table. She looked everywhere but at her friend. "You know how I feel about witches and magic. No good can come of this! Why did you never tell me?"

I did not know. "Edine, please…"

"Get out." Edine shook, then turned away, presenting her back and dropping her head. She sobbed, once. She cowered in fear. *Fear!*

Without trying to explain, without attempting to defend herself, Lyssa turned and ran.

Chapter Twelve

Blade found himself wishing that Lyssa would return from her friend's house sooner than she'd said she would. She was not needed here, not on such a quiet afternoon, but he still waited anxiously for her to walk through that door.

For the past two nights she had slept in their big bed alone, and he had slept before the fire in the main room. More rightly, he had attempted to sleep. He'd dozed, he'd dreamed, and he'd had to force himself to keep his distance.

Why? He did want Lyssa. That was undeniable. Though he had used the argument, he didn't stay away from her because he was afraid she might find herself with child. Not entirely, at least. That was already a possibility; one he could do nothing to change. In that bed, in her arms, he could see and feel the man he had become slipping away. He could feel his hate fading. In her bed, life became...good.

Blade had never imagined himself a shopkeeper. He didn't care for being indoors all day, for having a ceiling above his head rather than the sky, but working for Lyssa's father was not the huge sacrifice he'd expected it to be. People came and went all through the day, laughing and gossiping as they shopped. When Lyssa was there, he enjoyed watching her participate in lively discussions, and listening to her laugh. He even held his breath on occasion when she caught his eye for a long, torturous moment.

Without her present, the shop continued to function, but it was not as bright as it was when she was there.

As if she brought the sky inside with her. As if she was life itself. Foolish thought. Impossible.

If he'd believed he could sneak inside the palace and do what needed to be done without being caught before he killed Volker, he would have done it without a second thought. Living with Lyssa was painful in a way he had never imagined. What had seemed like a perfectly logical plan less than two weeks ago now seemed to him to be the most foolish decision he'd made in years…and he had made more than his share of foolish decisions in his lifetime.

Cyrus Tempest was a good man, a devoted husband and father, all in all a decent sort of fellow. But there were moments, snippets of time, when the shopkeeper looked at his daughter with an odd expression in his eyes, with an odd tension in the set of his shoulders. There was love, yes, but was that also…fear? Surely that was a misinterpretation.

Blade had thought, on more than one occasion, that Cyrus did not look after Lyssa as diligently as he should, but then, she was a grown woman and should not need a father to look out for her. A husband, however…*yes*.

Their marriage was not real. Not in any way that mattered. Legally they were man and wife. They shared a home, they had shared a bed, and dammit, he liked her.

But she affected him deeply in ways that he could not allow to continue. Marrying her, using her as his way into the palace, had turned into a complication. He could not afford to be distracted by her presence each and every day. He definitely could not afford to want her as desperately as he did, every night and every day. She was a means to an end and nothing more, but there were moments when it seemed as if they were creating so *much* more….

Another delivery would be made to the palace next week. Cyrus was awaiting a shipment of fabrics from the Northern Province, and a few were already promised to Empress Morgana. Blade could not imagine why anyone would need as much fabric as the empress apparently purchased, but if those purchases kept the Tempest shop healthy and Cyrus in enough coin to support his family, then who was he to care?

As ardently as Blade tried to dismiss his wife, he had been compelled to talk to Hagan, to make sure that no matter what happened, no matter what her father thought or did when the truth came out, Lyssa would have a home. He would not rest in peace if he didn't know she would be safe and well.

The time came to lock the doors of the shop, and still Lyssa had not returned from her friend's house. She'd said she would be back well before closing time, so where the hell was she?

"Lyssa should be here by now," Blade said. In spite of the worry growing inside him, he sounded more grumpy than concerned.

Cyrus shrugged his shoulders. "The girls probably lost track of time, or are in the middle of baking something and don't want to stop until they're done. Girls." The older man smiled as he shook his head. "Lyssa and Edine are girls no longer. They're women, fully grown and married." Standing outside the locked door of the shop, Cyrus looked up at Blade. "She's fine, I'm sure of it."

Blade was not sure. He didn't like this. He didn't like it at all. Something was wrong. He felt it in his gut where he usually felt nothing but hunger, anger, and a newly reignited desire. "Where is Edine's house?"

Cyrus pointed. "It's not far from here. Two streets down, one over, turn left. Her cottage has a bright blue

door. It's the only blue door on the street so you can't miss
it." With that Cyrus gave Blade a dismissive wave and said
goodbye. His own house and his own wife were right next
door, so he didn't have far to go.

Blade followed the directions he'd been given, his
strides long, his worry growing with each impatient step.
He didn't worry, not about things like this. He worried that
he would die before he killed Volker. He worried that his
soul had been tainted by murder—but not enough to regret
what he'd done. Lyssa was just a bit late, and that was not a
reason for concern. And yet, he could not walk fast enough.
Soon he was knocking on a blue door, wondering why he
had felt compelled to come here, why he had not just gone
home and waited. It wasn't as if Lyssa couldn't find her way
there on her own.

His knock was answered with a sharp cry. "Who's
there?"

The hairs on the back of his neck stood up in warning.
That was not a happy response. And it was not Lyssa.
"Blade Renshaw. I'm looking for my wife."

The door opened a crack a few seconds later, and
Edine peeked around the edge of the blue door. Her face
was pale, her eyes wide. "Lyssa is a witch," she whispered.
"I never knew. I don't think she did, either. Did *you* know,
when you married her?"

"Don't be ridiculous," Blade said, defending Lyssa
even as his mind recounted all the unusual events of the
past weeks, including the fact that she had never answered
him when he'd asked her straight out if she was a witch.

Edine poked a hand through the opening in the door
and presented a perfectly ordinary palm. "I cut myself.
Deep. Blood was everywhere, but Lyssa healed it with a
touch."

Lyssa had talked about mending an old woman's knee, and while he'd tried to dismiss all the things she claimed to know…all these things together painted a clear picture. Magic existed. It always had. And while magic was not prevalent by any means, most accepted it without fear unless a half-demon was involved. But there were still some—ignorant fools—who were frightened of *all* magic. Edine was obviously one of them.

"I should think you would be grateful that she healed you of a serious injury."

"You know nothing of magic," Edine cried, clearly agitated. "One who can heal can also wound. Two sides of the same coin, two aspects of the same magic. No unnatural power comes free! There is a cost, always. A price to pay. I love Lyssa, she was my best friend…."

Was. "But you are afraid of her now."

"Yes," she whispered.

"Where is she?"

"I don't know." With that, Edine slammed the door in Blade's face. From beyond the blue door he heard a sob and a soft, "I'm sorry, so sorry. Oh, God, what have I done?"

He turned away from the house, from the foolish woman in it, and took two steps toward the cottage he'd called home since taking a wife. But then he stopped dead still in the middle of the street. She was not there. He knew it without doubt.

With a sharp about-face, he headed away from the palace that sat at the center of Arthes, away from the cottage Lyssa should have fled to when she'd left her friend.

Blade took long strides, and soon he was running. He should not know in which direction Lyssa had run, but he did. He should not care, but he did. Witch? Yes. *More?*

Without a doubt.

Lyssa sat on the soft ground and leaned against a tree. She was out of breath, her eyes burned after shedding far too many tears, and her heart was pounding so hard she could feel it. She'd torn the hem of her dress not long after entering the forest, and along the way had dragged that hem through the mud. Her hair had fallen from its once neat style, and strands fell over her eyes and across her cheeks, but she didn't bother to brush them away.

She hadn't seen anyone since entering the forest at a run, not looking back, not understanding why the shadows and the trees called to her. The thicker and darker the woods became, the harder she ran. All she could think of was escape. She'd fled the city, fled Blade's rejection and Edine's hate. She'd run until she could not run any more, until her legs ached and she could hardly breathe.

Where was she? She'd left the boundaries of Arthes a while back, had run into the woods as if she were being chased by wild animals rather than her own fears, and now…now darkness was approaching, closing in on her, and she could not walk another step, much less run any more.

There was so much green all around, dark green and light, new growth and old. Some of the trees that grew here were ancient, so old she could not even begin to guess how many years they had survived in this forest. Others were new, fragile and wispy. She stepped carefully over gnarled roots that rose up out of the ground, and finally leaned against a tree. It was as good a place as any to stop, she imagined. She sank to the ground and leaned her back against the solid trunk.

There was color here, as well as an abundance of green. There were red berries and yellow wildflowers. The occasional butterfly.

Edine, the best friend Lyssa had ever known, was afraid of her. She would never forget the expression on her friend's face, the horror, the disbelief....It had been worse than a physical blow. Was that why Blade did not want to touch her again? Was *he* afraid of her, too? Being alone would be better than this, better than being feared by those she loved, being cast out because she had powers she could not explain. The power to heal was a fine one, was it not? So why was everyone afraid of her?

Maybe because they, like she, didn't know what other powers waited just beneath the surface.

Since the age of fifteen, every decision she'd made had been colored by Vellance's dire prediction. *Alone.* Her father and Sinmora. Edine. Blade. She had tried to use them all to ensure that she would never be alone, but the truth was, she had no one. Her father and Sinmora had each other, and their baby. Edine had her family, as all Lyssa's other friends had families. Like her, Blade had no one. Unlike her, he wanted no one.

All she'd ever desired was a normal life. Love, a family, a quiet existence. A home, laughter at the end of the day, someone to lean upon in bad times and celebrate with in good. She could have none of that...not now. She was a witch, and no one would ever love her, not the way she wanted to be loved. When her father and Sinmora found out what she was, they wouldn't want her in their home, wouldn't want her around their child. Just like Edine, they would be afraid.

She would end up like Vellance, living in the forest, begging strangers for assistance, scaring those she met with dire predictions and toothless smiles. Perhaps now and then she would meet someone who needed healing, and she would use the gift she'd found. But once they'd benefitted from her ability, those she healed wouldn't want her anywhere near them. Like Edine.

Of everyone she knew, Edine was the one person she had never expected to hurt her....

Lyssa heard Blade coming long before he called her name, knew without doubt that it was him thrashing through the forest and scaring away all the small creatures. The larger ones, too. He was moving straight to her, drawn by the bond they shared, though he did not know it. He had been called into the forest because she had unknowingly trapped him with her witch's powers. Blade was compelled not by love or friendship or caring but by magic. Dark or light? How was she to know? She had not asked for this. It was just *there*.

She should hide. Well, she could *try*. Could she hide from Blade, or would he find her wherever she went? Day or night, forest or city...he would be drawn to her.

"I'm sorry," she whispered, long before he was close enough to hear her. "I did not know."

She didn't move from her place at the base of the tree, only sat and waited. When Blade stepped around a thick-trunked tree and saw her, he stopped and stared down with what looked to be concern on his face. It wasn't real concern, though. It was magic. She had bound this husband to her, captured him as surely as if she'd manacled him to her bed. He breathed hard; his eyes were narrowed. No bond or magic was necessary for her to discern that he was annoyed that she'd drawn him all the way out here, away from his quest, away from the scheme that had brought them together.

"There's something very wrong with me," she said.

He stepped closer and offered her a hand. A big, warm, strong hand. She did not take it, tempting as it was. "Come along," he said. "It will soon be dark."

Lyssa shook her head and looked down at her knees. "I can't go back. Everyone will know what I am. If not now, then...it won't be long. Edine will tell, and Madam Azar will hear and then she'll tell everyone about her knee, and...and everyone will hate me. I will be alone, just as the witch said. It was not enough to marry before I turned twenty-three. I did something wrong." Or else there had never been a chance for her, and the witch Vellance had simply offered false hope.

She thought Blade might try to force her to stand, that he might grab her and pull her to her feet and throw her over his shoulder...but instead he sat beside her. Close. He was tired and muddy, too. Maybe he just wanted to rest a moment before heading back to town.

"I'm sorry you came all this way for nothing," she whispered.

He was quiet for a moment—catching his breath, she imagined—and then he asked, "Where will you go?"

"I don't know." Maybe she would just sit here until a wolf devoured her or she starved to death. No, thirst would get her before starvation. She wasn't sure about the wolves. Were they close? In the past several years, she'd heard them howling in the distance as she'd tried to go to sleep, but as she'd been safe in her bed at the time she hadn't given them much thought. Their howling was simply a vague and distant part of the night. Not a danger, not something to be afraid of. Not until now.

Blade sat with her as the day faded and the shadows all around grew deeper. She kept expecting him to stand, tell her goodbye, and head back to Arthes. But long after his breathing had returned to normal he remained.

Putting aside every fear, letting go of the nightmares that had plagued her sleep for the past eight years, Lyssa lifted her chin with hard-won—and fragile—courage and said, "You are free to go. I don't need you."

She expected him to stand quickly and make his escape. Maybe he would even thank her for letting him go. It would be the polite thing to do. But instead he said, instantly and decisively, "No. I will not leave you here."

Stubborn man! "Well, I can't go back," she said logically.

"I didn't ask you to."

How could he sound so calm?

She reached for an unknown reserve of strength. "I release you from any and all obligation. Go."

Again he said, "No."

She looked directly at him then, exasperated, terrified—and more than a little relieved. The night was rapidly growing dark, and she wished she could see his face more clearly so she could read his expression. He was a shadow, much like the other shadows of the forest, the shadows of the coming night. "Why on earth would you stay?"

He didn't answer that question, but he did speak. "I know a man in the Southern Province who lives near the sea. It's not the village where I once lived, but it is nearby. I repaired this man's boat long ago, and we became friends of a sort. There are not many people in his village. They fish and grow the few crops that can thrive there. It would be a good place for us to go, at least for now."

She looked up at him, again wishing she could see his face. Was he teasing her? Torturing her? "Us?"

"I cannot let you go on alone."

Words she'd once longed to hear, but now…now she understood that it would be wrong to do this to him. "You can. It's magic that binds you to me, nothing more. Maybe with distance between us…" She let the sentence remain unfinished. It was impossible to say aloud that with distance what she thought was love and he thought was obligation would simply fade away.

"It's more than magic, Lyssa." He sounded positively disgruntled. "When I thought you were gone, when I was running through the woods wondering if I would find you, if I would ever see you again, I knew that if I *did* find you I would never let you go. You were not in my plans. You took me by surprise—you take me by surprise every day— but I will not let you go."

It was everything she'd ever wanted from a man and nothing she'd ever expected from Blade. "What about your revenge? The man in the palace…?"

"He will still be there when this is done."

"When what is done?"

He waited several long seconds before answering. "I'm not sure."

She rested her head on his shoulder, glad of his warmth and his strength. "I'm sorry I did this to you. I didn't mean to…I didn't…When I married you, I…I didn't know."

He didn't claim not to understand what she was talking about.

Princess stood at the window and looked out into the night, as she so often did. She preferred night to day, dark to light. Her sisters were still awake tonight. They were all on edge, and she knew why.

"The witch and the blade are farther away now," she said without turning to look at them.

"Isn't that a good thing?" Divya asked.

Princess liked Divya. Divya was a real sister to her, but she did not always care for the other. Runa was a demon daughter, a Ksana demon, but she was too soft, too uncertain about who and what she was. And Princess was almost certain that Runa sometimes hid her thoughts. That should be impossible. The Ksana demons should be unable to hide anything—thoughts, emotions, power—from each other. But Runa held back, somehow.

She might have to die before the war began. It was possible she could not be trusted.

"No, it's not a good thing," Princess snapped. "Together they will both grow stronger. If either one were to die the other would wither, but if they're out of reach there's nothing to be done."

"Perhaps our Father will allow us to go free so we can hunt them down ourselves," Divya suggested. She clapped her hands in glee at the thought. "It will be a great adventure."

Princess realized—too late, of course—that she should have escaped when she'd had the chance, that night she'd fed from the sentinel outside their prison door. At that time she'd still believed that the man who called himself Father wanted and needed her. She'd still believed that he was a part of the plan to bring to her all the power she desired.

Now she was not so sure. "I doubt that he will release us for any reason. He does not trust us. Not entirely." More than that, Volker was afraid of the girls he called his daughters. He was afraid that one day they would suck the life force from his body.

He was not necessarily wrong.

The longer Princess remained in this room, the stronger she grew. With every passing day knowledge came to her, truths of the world beyond these walls were revealed. There were other demon daughters—Ksana and not Ksana—here and elsewhere. Strong and weak, near and far, dark and...darker. Their powers were varied, and yet they did share a bond. A few, a mere handful, had been ruined by white magic, by love and light. They were rare, these infected demon daughters, and of no concern to Princess. They would die soon enough.

Some of them, again just a few, also called Miron Volker *Father*. There were even those he loved more than her. A few days ago she had thought that to be impossible, but...as knowledge came to her, as the truth was revealed in dreams as well as in waking hours, she came to understand that he was using her, using her and her sisters as he used mortal men and those who possessed a more ordinary magic than her own. Some Volker bound to him with love; others wanted gold or power, or both.

What did *she* want? The answer to that question was easy. She wanted everything.

There was great power in the knowledge she had acquired just tonight, knowledge that had come to her as she looked out upon the world. She should have realized sooner, should have known...

Volker needed her and her sisters much more than they needed him.

Chapter Thirteen

Blade accepted without question that he would be dead by now if not for Lyssa. It was what he'd planned, what he'd *wanted*. Maybe he would have finished Volker before he'd died, and maybe he would have died before accomplishing his mission, but he *would* be dead.

But tonight, he was alive, and since it was too dark for them to try to travel he'd collected edible nuts and berries for a simple supper, and then they'd walked to a nearby stream to drink hands full of cool water. Fed, they'd settled down by the tree where he'd found Lyssa. They had both run from Arthes unprepared, with no food, no blankets, not even an empty tin cup. Thank goodness he always wore his dagger; he'd feel helpless without it. It wasn't much, but if they were going to spend several days walking toward the sea, he was glad not to be traveling unarmed.

Lyssa soon slept, exhausted by both physical and emotional strain. For a long while Blade lay awake, but eventually he fell into a restless sleep disturbed by dreams that seemed more real than not.

Hagan was there, in his dream, and so was Volker. Blade's blood ran cold when he confronted Volker in his nightmare. He felt intense pain when Volker thrust a sword into his heart. It was a rusty sword, Blade thought as he died, and then he realized that it wasn't rusted but was stained with the blood of another. Runa's blood. No, he realized in a panic, his mind spinning, that was Lyssa's blood. Her vision of him killing Volker had been wrong, very wrong.

And then the dream shifted and Lyssa was there. Alive, warm, touching him and whispering in his ear. She told him that she loved him, and he believed her, and then she told him that she wanted him. He believed *that*, too. His wife was almost impossible to resist in the waking world, but here, in his dreams, why should he turn his back on what he wanted?

She smelled and felt real and good, even in a dream. They kissed and touched, and held onto one another tightly in the darkness, as if together they could create their own light and fight the dark.

Gradually Blade realized that this was no dream. It was real, warm, everything he wanted and everything he did not. Lyssa freed his erection, caressed it with gentle fingers, and then she pushed him onto his back and straddled him. Wet and tight and hot, she lowered herself onto his length and rode him. She gasped, and made those little noises deep in her throat, noises that drove him mad, that made him want her more.

She moved slowly at first, easily, then faster. Harder. Because he was unable to see, their joining was pure physical sensation, powerful and pleasurable. He felt her everywhere, around him, inside him in a way different from the way he was inside her.

In the same way she had healed Edine's hand and an old woman's knee, she was healing him. His pain was not as simple as a cut or a rusty joint, so the healing had taken some time. But the result was the same. Every time he touched her, every time he held or kissed or laid with her, she healed a piece of his heart. His soul. She took away the hate that had driven him for so long, and he could not allow that to happen, because that hate was all he had left.

That hate was who he had become. He fought the healing, fought *her*. Why could he not keep his pleasure *and* his pain? Why could he not have Lyssa *and* his revenge?

She cried out, quivered around him, and he climaxed with her. For a moment he thought that maybe, real as she felt, this was a dream after all. Real life could not be so perfect.

Lyssa woke with a soft ray of sun in her eyes. It took her a moment to get oriented, to remember where she was. In the forest, on the run, sleeping with her head on Blade's chest. She lay with her face directly in the path of a narrow strip of morning sun that found its way through the heavy growth above.

They were both as much undressed as dressed, clothing askew, bodies still entangled. She remembered last night with a smile. They had made love. She liked those words much more than the other one. Maybe that love was created by magic, and maybe it wouldn't last, but for now she would take it. That love was all she had. It was the only love she would ever know.

Blade woke, smiled at her with a strip of morning's soft sunlight on his own face…but that smile did not last.

"What have you done to me?" he asked.

She drew away from him. They were both rumpled and dirty. Blade had a few dead leaves in his hair, and she supposed she did, too. A few leaves were probably the least of her problems at the moment. Maybe she wasn't the most beautiful bride in the world, but was she so hideous that she incited pure horror in her husband? "What did I do to you? What did *you* do to *me*?"

"At first I thought it was a dream," he said softly, as he took in her state of dishevelment.

"I assure you, it was *not*." What had she been thinking? Simple. She'd awakened in the middle of a dark night, afraid and uncertain, and so relieved not to be alone. Blade had been right *there*, and she had wanted him—as she always wanted him—and it had just happened. No real thinking had been required.

Until Blade had made her his wife, she'd had no idea what a true joining with another could be like. It was the sex and more; it was a feeling of connection she had never imagined, not even when she'd so feared living her life alone. If she had not gone to the tavern that night, if she had decided that a nunnery was the path for her, she never would have known the depths of true pleasure. She never would have known true love, and so she never would have missed it. How could one miss what one did not understand?

Should she thank Blade or curse him? Without him, she never would have realized what truly being alone could be. To have this and lose it…Maybe she'd be better off if she didn't understand what she was leaving behind.

Blade sat up and straightened his clothing so he was relatively decent. Then he put his head in his hands and just sat there, discouraged and…and…heartbroken, she realized.

"Was making love to your wife so horrible?" she snapped. She tried to push back the tears that gathered in her eyes, tried to hide her pain. "Am I repulsive to you?"

He looked at her, his blue eyes solemn. She had seen him angry and determined and laughing in spite of himself, but she had never really seen him look sad. Not like this. "You are not repulsive, Lyssa. You are beautiful and passionate, and any man would be glad to have you as a wife."

She refrained from laughing out loud at *that* lie. Bad Luck Lyssa. Terrible Tempest. She did not want their conversation to go there. "Any man but you, apparently." She stood, brushed off her skirt, and straightened her blouse. "I need to relieve myself, and then I'll head south. You should not feel obligated to accompany me." She stalked away from him with her head high, and then, with her back to him so he could not see, she allowed the tears to fall. Silently, of course. She would not sob in his presence.

She'd married a stranger to ensure that she would never be alone, and yet now she *chose* a solitary life. She *chose* to travel on her own. To be alone had seemed so horrible to her, so...well, lonely. And yet there were worse fates than solitude. She knew that now. To love and not be loved in return, to become something she did not understand...

When she returned to the tree, Blade was still there. Standing, spine straight, his clothing had been returned to its proper state. Like her, he was a bit worse for wear, but he was also...beautiful.

"We should go back into the city," he said, "collect some food and weapons and—"

"No," she interrupted before he could say more, a shiver walking up her spine. "It isn't safe for us to go back. Not yet."

"Why?"

A simple question for which she did not have a simple answer. Just last night she had tried to send him back, but now she knew it was not a safe place for either of them. The red-eyed demon was there, but...was that the only danger? She suspected not, but her magic was new, imperfect…maddening. "I don't understand why, but it's truth."

He did not argue with her. Already he had accepted that she knew things she should not. He accepted that she was a witch. No wonder he'd looked so horrified upon waking!

"You can go anywhere else but Arthes, but it is not safe for you to go there now. She wants to kill you." She turned and walked away. He followed.

"Who wants to kill me?"

"The same creature who wants to kill me," she said sharply. "A Ksana demon, as I told you before. That's all I see. It's all I know. It's maddening to see so little, to know bits and pieces and not be able to see the whole picture. Now go." Without turning to look at him, she waved one hand dismissively and kept walking. He did not leave but remained directly behind her.

"No one will kill you while I'm around," he said, sounding determined for a man who had been so distressed to face the morning's truth that he'd made love to her. Again.

"I don't need you."

"Yes, you do." His long strides brought him close to her, closer than she wanted him to be. How was she supposed to cry with him *right there*?

"I do not want you!"

"Liar," he said without heat.

She wasn't blind or stupid. Naive on occasion, yes, but not stupid. Blade would prefer to embrace his hate than to love her. She knew him well enough to understand that he was terrified to think that she might take that hate away with her touch. With her love. With her body. Where did that leave them? How could she remain with him and not make love to him?

No, those words were wrong. Edine's husband's crude "poke" was more appropriate for what happened between her and her husband. At least, that was what she told herself as she tried to be strong. Admitting that love existed would make her weak, and she could not afford weakness. Not now.

Nothing else was working, so she lied, again, in a more temperate tone of voice. "Truly, Blade, I do not want you. I prefer to travel alone."

"That's too damn bad, because you're not going anywhere without me."

He didn't love her; he didn't care. Magic bound him to her; witch's magic. When the opportunity came for her to slip away from him, she would. Perhaps with some distance between them, the magical connection would face away and he would be free. Free to hate, free to seek his revenge.

Free to die.

Miron Volker had duties as Minister of Foreign Affairs; annoying, insignificant duties that too often took him away from his true calling. His entire focus should be on marshaling his own army, as well as collecting half-demon girls and ensuring that they needed him.

When he did rule, no one would be able to topple him the way he intended to topple Emperor Jahn.

Bothersome as they were, his duties as Minister allowed him free run of the palace, so he would endure them. It would not be for much longer.

Stasio interrupted Volker as he was making plans for the upcoming trip to Tryfyn. The man in the black robes had been incredibly helpful, but there were moments when Volker was certain the wizard wanted more than a subservient position. One day Stasio would need to be eliminated, he suspected. But not today.

"I'm going ahead this afternoon," Stasio said. He should have asked, not told, but Volker did not correct the other man. "I believe there is at least one extremely powerful half Anwyn demon child near the Tryfyn capital. She would make an excellent addition to your army."

Half wolf-shifter and half Isen Demon? There were other demon shifters, he knew. He already had one in his possession; a thin, dark-haired girl who shifted into a large cat at will and was also quite the talented seer. But to possess a daughter with true Anwyn blood...If such a creature existed, he wanted her.

If the Isen Demon's warriors had been able to produce male children, what would they be like? More trouble than they'd be worth, Volker imagined. Girls were easier for him to manipulate, whether they were poisonous Ksanas or powerful shifters or simply possessed some odd bit of magic. There was still so much to be learned about the Isen Demon's offspring. So much power and beauty to be discovered.

"Should I provide an escort?" Volker asked? Woe be to any thief who thought to rob or injure the wizard before him, but Volker wanted to make sure that Stasio felt valued. That he warranted a handful of sentinels to guard him on his travels.

"That won't be necessary."

"Good," Volker said to his second in command. "I'll see you in two weeks, then."

Stasio did not leave, though Volker's words were definitely a dismissal. "Your Princess has been asking for you."

"I have other concerns at the moment." Volker looked down at the papers on his desk, studying his itinerary for the upcoming trip.

"She says the witch and the blade are making their escape. They are moving away from Arthes."

Wasn't that a good thing?

As if Stasio had read his mind—and perhaps he had—the wizard went on. "They will only grow stronger if not stopped now."

Volker stood, and in frustration slapped his palms against his desk and leaned forward. "Why are my girls so afraid of a mortal man and a common witch?"

Stasio shrugged his shoulders. "I do not know, but they *are*, and when I meditate and reach for truth, I sense great power in the witch."

Until now, Volker had been quick to dismiss the girls' worries about the witch and the blade. He had so much on his mind. But if Stasio sensed great power…perhaps there would be a use for it in the coming days. Could this witch also become a part of his army? Could he use her? "How do you suggest we proceed?"

Expressionless, as always, Stasio gave a quick bow. "As it happens, I have a plan in mind."

In spite of her bad memories of the forest and the witch who had frightened her on the road so long ago, Lyssa found beauty as they traveled south. Everything was so green, and colorful flowers grew in the most unlikely places. More than yellow, here. Purple and white and red, too. She didn't see much in the way of wildlife; just a few butterflies and small birds and one brave rabbit—which looked delicious, she had to admit—but she did, on occasion, hear rustling leaves as something larger than a rabbit moved away.

As long as it moved *away* and not toward…

She was thankful that she'd been wearing sturdy boots instead of her pretty slippers when she'd instinctively run away from Edine. Her moss green dress was torn and dirty, her hair was in tangles, and her stomach growled in hunger…but her boots were holding up well. If she expired along the way, a bag of muddy bones and a hank of unmanageable hair, at least her footwear would be intact.

Her stubborn husband remained behind her, walking silently in her wake. She'd tried to send him away—for his own good—but he ignored her and continued to follow, keeping his distance.

Why? He did not love her, of that she was certain. Did he still see her as his way into the palace? Did he plan to use her newfound magic to take his revenge? This would be so much easier if she had not fallen in love with him, if he was just a thief and a murderer, a man who had no use for her but for his own revenge.

But there was more to him, more than even he knew.

After a while he moved closer. There was nothing to be done about that, since his legs were much longer than hers and she could not out-walk or outrun him.

"We need to find something to eat," he said.

"I'm not hungry." At that precise moment her stomach growled loudly.

He had the good sense not to point out her body's reaction to the word *eat*. "We have a long walk ahead of us, and we must have food. If you had let me go back for provisions…"

"No." She stopped, spun to look at him. "It isn't safe for either of us to return to Arthes. I told you that." When she thought of turning back she saw blood. Lots of it. She couldn't tell whose blood it was, but the very thought of it—this new vision of blood that occasionally formed in her mind as she walked—turned her stomach and made her want to scream.

"I believe you," Blade said. "Now, sit and rest while I round up some food."

Why not do as he said? Her legs ached and her feet hurt a little, so she walked to a nearby rock and sat. Frightened, hopelessly rumpled, and with no idea of what tomorrow might bring, she straightened her spine and lifted her chin, and sat in as ladylike a position as she could manage. Blade smiled at her—he *smiled*—and then he ordered her to stay put while he disappeared beyond a stand of trees in search of sustenance.

For a moment she thought about taking the opportunity to run, but what was the point? He would find her, as he had found her yesterday.

And in spite of everything…she still did not want to be alone.

Nuts, berries, wild greens he knew to be edible…considering their situation, it was a veritable feast, though they would soon need meat to keep up their strength. He'd even hollowed out a fallen branch and filled it with spring water, so that Lyssa did not have to walk down the hill to the spring to drink from her cupped hands. She was tired. Terrified, angry, lost…and exhausted. It was his duty to care for her, to watch over her.

To save her as he had not been able to save his mother or his sister. He would not be late again; he would not let Lyssa out of his sight from this point forward.

That didn't mean he'd given up his quest to kill Miron Volker, it just meant his plans would have to be delayed. But for how long? He had no idea.

More. Lyssa had said that together they were more. Like it or not, he had begun to believe that she was right. His world was larger than it had been when he'd arrived in Arthes with no goal but to kill Volker. It was also more complicated, but there was nothing to be done about that. It seemed more urgent, right now, to explore this new possibility with Lyssa.

She devoured the nuts and berries, and nibbled at the greens. She drank from the crudely fashioned cup, and then she sighed and lifted her eyes to him.

"You really can go," she said softly. "Not back to Arthes, but…I do not want you to feel obligated to take care of me. I can find my own way to the sea and from there…"

"From there *what*?" he asked when she faltered.

"I don't know. One step at a time."

Blade stood, brushed some dirt from his trousers and then offered Lyssa his hand. After a brief hesitation, she took it, and he pulled her to her feet. Cupping her face in his palms, he looked deep into her eyes and said sternly, "You are my wife, and I will not let you loose in this forest, or on any road, or in any village."

"But…"

"I don't know if I make you more than you were or not, but you have awakened something in me that I can't deny. If anything happened to you, I would never forgive myself." That was the raw truth. He didn't have to like it, because his feelings didn't change anything.

"It's not like we're truly man and wife. We—"

"We were married by a priest, the marriage was consummated, and we have lived together in our own home. No couple is more truly man and wife than we are."

"I do wish you would stop interrupting me."

"Am I wrong?"

She bit her bottom lip, briefly, as she considered her answer. "No, you are not wrong, but neither of us intended for this marriage to be real. I know very well you did not plan to keep me. You used me."

"*You* used *me*." He leaned in and kissed the side of her neck. "Intentions aside, we are man and wife. Perhaps…perhaps I will survive and decide to keep you."

Her breath came hard all of a sudden. Her heart pounded, as it always did when he was close. He felt her reaction because they were so close, because he knew her so well.

"Why?" she asked. "Why would you even think to keep me?"

"Because I desire to do so." He wanted to live, to make babies with Lyssa, to sleep with her every night. He wasn't certain he could make that happen, but he wanted it—badly. He also wanted Volker dead. That had not changed. Could he have everything he wanted? Was that possible?

He took Lyssa's face in his hands and made her look him in the eye. "There's something I must tell you. You have to know why I can't let Volker go."

She nodded once. " Volker, that's the name of the man you traveled so far to kill. He murdered your sister." Her words were gentle, a comfort and a caress.

"Yes." Blade set his jaw. The pain never lessened, and he had to fight to say the words. They came out in a growl. "She was eleven years old."

Lyssa gasped.

"And she was one of the demon's children."

She leaned into him, placed her head on his chest and wrapped her arms around his waist. No words would heal such a deep and terrible pain, so she offered none, but her touch was a comfort.

He didn't push her away, but instead accepted the closeness, the offered comfort. And when they parted he once again took her face in his hands, and his mouth descended onto hers. He had not intended to kiss her, but she was right there and he needed that touch.

She kissed him back, parted her lips and brushed the tip of her tongue against his. Silent, telling tears ran down her face. These salty tears he tasted were not tears of sadness or anger. These tears stemmed from power, from beauty.

There was desperation in their kiss, passion and pain and longing. But there was also something else. Something that might be called love.

Chapter Fourteen

Blade walked beside her now, instead of behind as he had earlier in the day. Lyssa liked it; she liked being able to reach out and touch him if she felt as if she might stumble. And they'd been walking for such a long time that stumbling was a definite possibility.

She'd never expected that he might care for her, but he seemed to. He'd never used the word "love," but then neither had she. Not aloud, anyway. But he was here. He'd stayed even though she had tried to send him away. Was it really magic that kept him with her? Or could he actually be basing his decision on free will? If she had to be a witch, she wished she could control whatever powers she might possess. It would be nice to know what was in his mind and his heart.

She was dirty and her hair was a mess, and still he had kissed her after he'd told her about his sister. It had been an amazing kiss. A real kiss. Surely there was some sort of magic involved. Why else would he want to kiss her when she was so incredibly unattractive? Last night's lovemaking could be excused, since it had been dark and he hadn't been able to see any better than she had, but to kiss her by the light of day, to stay with her in spite of who and what she was…

Why had he not shunned her as Edine had done? Why wouldn't he take the opportunity to be rid of her? She had the uneasy suspicion that it must be some sort of witch's magic that was beyond her control.

They walked some distance from the well-traveled road, but had found themselves on a rough path of sorts. It lead them in the right direction, or so Blade insisted, and the travel was easier than if they had tried to forge their own trail. They were surrounded by ancient trees that towered above them and younger trees struggling to find the sun. Earlier they had encountered some gentle hills, and Lyssa was grateful that the path was now relatively flat. They passed the occasional clearing that revealed signs of other travelers. The remnants of a fire here; the bones of a long ago supper there. They saw no one. That was no surprise, as most travelers would stick with the road. Birds and small animals rustled the leaves of trees and low bushes; she had stopped jumping at every sound a while back.

Blade talked about what he might catch for their evening meal and where they might camp for the night. Lyssa listened, but she was distracted. Her thoughts were solidly on her husband, on magic, and witchcraft. And on that kiss...

Without even a whisper of warning, four large men wearing sentinels' uniforms stepped out of the woods. Lyssa was frozen on the path, shocked into stillness, but Blade reacted instantly. He threw himself toward her, protecting her from the first attacker, a stocky man who moved on her in complete and unnatural silence. The attackers' boots made no noise on the forest floor; she did not hear any of the men breathe, didn't hear even a rustle of clothing. It was like a bad dream, so much so that for a second she wondered if maybe she'd fallen asleep and none of this was real.

No, this was far too real.

Blade had a knife; she had a newfound magic she did not understand and could not control. The four men who surrounded them had swords, shining blades that did not belong in the quiet safety of the forest, and at this moment the power of their weapons seemed to be stronger, more real, than any magic she might muster.

Blade's much-too-short dagger should have been all but worthless against the sword that swung in their direction, but it was not. He moved with an almost unnatural quickness and grace. As he fought, feinting and stabbing and trying to draw blood and drive the silent man back, another moved toward her. But Blade was fast, and he was strong. He defended her against two simultaneous attackers surprisingly well, drawing blood and keeping the attackers' blades away from her.

But then the other two moved in, and the balance of power changed. Blade could fight against two, but four…He had no chance against four men with swords. Trained fighters who made no sound as they moved…

Until Lyssa touched them. One soldier grabbed her from behind while Blade pushed another back, and suddenly she heard a boot among fallen leaves, heavy breathing. Her healing power had lifted whatever dark magic gave the swordsman the gift of silence.

Once she realized that her touch robbed them of their magical silence, she attempted to lay her hands on them all to ensure that Blade could hear when one of them moved behind him. But that knowledge and her actions came too late, and the ability to hear them was not enough to outweigh their advantage in number and in weaponry. Blade drew blood, but so did they. His arm, his thigh, and finally his torso, very near his heart.

She watched as a sentinel's blade pierced his chest. Blood bloomed on his shirt, quick and dark. He fell, and Lyssa heard herself scream as one of the attackers grabbed the back of her dress and pulled her away.

She managed to wrench herself from his grasp and fall to the ground, her hands splaying on Blade's chest. There was so much blood, and he was so still…was he already dead? No, no, his chest rose and fell. His heart beat beneath her hands; it had not been pierced by an attacker's sword.

"I love you," she whispered, pressing both hands to his chest. She'd never tried to heal before, not like this. Madam Azar's knee had been entirely accidental. The healing of Edine's hand had been instinctive. In both cases the healing had been quick, almost instantaneous, but neither of those wounds had been like this one. Deep. A killing wound. She searched for the green light and had almost found it when one of the attackers grabbed her by the hair and pulled her to her feet. She was dragged away from Blade, her bloody hands ripped from his chest.

He needed her. At last she could help him with the magic she'd found. She could save him if only she could touch him. One more time.

"Please, let me say goodbye to my husband," she pleaded as she stumbled back, falling clumsily into the man who held onto her tightly, too tightly. "He's dying!" She had barely touched him. Was it enough?

"No," the man who dragged her away said. "We have our orders."

"From who? What kind of orders?" Her heart thudded dangerously hard and her breath would barely come. "I'm no one. I'm nothing!" Blade was getting farther and farther away. She could no longer tell if he was breathing or not. He didn't move, not even a twitch of a finger. "Why are you doing this?"

No one answered her. The stocky man dragged her away from the path, away from Blade. She tried to fight, but the man who had captured her was strong, solid. Her struggles were useless. She screamed. Once, twice. At first the sentinels seemed not to care, and then one of them—she could not see his face—said in a passionless voice that if her screams drew anyone to them, if anyone tried to help her, the would-be rescuers would be killed as her husband had been killed.

Lyssa believed the threat. She had no doubt about their potential for violence, so she went silent. She tried to walk, as they led her toward the road she and Blade had been avoiding, but her steps were too short and the solid man continued to drag her along. She was panting by the time they reached a clearing where five horses waited. One for her and one for each of them, she noted. Had they intended for Blade to share a horse with her or walk? No, they had never intended for him to survive to this point. They had intended all along to kill him.

She breathed deeply when she was finally allowed to stop. Her head spun, tears trailed down her cheeks and still her heart pounded too hard. But she didn't have very long to mourn Blade or feel sorry for herself. Her hands were bound, a rough gag was fashioned over her mouth, and she was unceremoniously and roughly thrown over a horse's saddle. She had not begged for mercy for herself, and it was too late to beg for Blade. But as she landed on the saddle, hard and rough, a new thought flashed through her head.

Don't hurt my baby.

Blade could feel the ground beneath him, but he could not move. He was dead, had realized he was dead as soon as the sentinel's sword had sliced into him that last time and torn his insides apart.

Was there pain in the Land of the Dead? Was this searing hurt to be his eternal punishment for the wrongs he'd done in his living years?

A soft voice whispered in his ear. No, in his *head*. *Find me.* Runa beyond death or Lyssa in the Land of the Living? He was in between lives, he knew, in between the two women he loved. His sister and his wife. He had failed them both. It took great effort, but he opened his eyes. There, standing over him, was a girl dressed all in white. She was not quite solid, not quite...there. It took him a moment to recognize her, it had been so long. Runa. Runa as she would have been if she'd lived. Fifteen years old. As pretty as their mother had been, before time and war and soldiers had taken her beauty from her. So, he was dead after all.

"Not yet," she whispered, as if she had read his mind. "Not for a very long time."

"Runa..."

"Find her, Blade. Save her and your daughter...."

"I don't have a daughter."

Runa smiled. "You will."

With that his little sister was gone, and the pain returned with a vengeance. He closed his eyes, squeezed them shut. "Come back," he whispered. He had so many questions for her, so much to say.

Again he opened his eyes. The hazy world spun and in response he pressed his hands into the dirt to make it stop. He was on his back in the forest. Sitting up was an effort, but he managed. He looked around for Lyssa, for the attackers. All he saw were the signs of a bloody struggle. He glanced down at his torn and bloody clothes, lifted a scrap of blood-stained fabric to look at the place on his chest where a blade had sliced through his flesh. He had to wipe away drying blood—how long had be been lying here?

How long since he'd dreamed of Runa?—but there was no wound. There was not even a scar, other than the one Volker had given him four years ago. He checked the cuts on his arm, the gash on his leg, and found the same. Blood and torn clothing, but no actual wounds.

Lyssa. Lyssa had healed him. His wife, his witch, the woman who had made him more from the moment she'd looked into his eyes.

Blade placed a hand over his heart. Dammit, she had healed him there, too, though he had fought against it with all he possessed. The need for vengeance that had given him purpose was gone. It was as if there was a hole where a part of him had been, as if she had not healed him so much as ripped away a piece of his soul.

But a new need had taken the place of that once-nurtured hatred. Blade now had a burning need to save the woman he loved and the daughter they had made, or would make. Even if his vision of Runa had been a fever dream, he knew that he and Lyssa would have babies. Daughters, like her. Sons…again, more like her than like him, he could hope, though they would be his to teach. To train.

He had not come back from the dead to walk away from his wife.

Blade couldn't say if what he felt for her was real or if it was created by magic. Until he saw her safe, it did not matter.

He searched the forest floor around him. His dagger was gone. He didn't want to move forward without a weapon of any kind, but he would if he had to. Maybe one of the attackers had dropped a sword and he would finally have the weapon Lyssa had assured him he would use to kill Volker.

But no. No sword.

Blade crawled forward, brushing aside fallen leaves, continuing to search. His dagger was nearby, he knew it. Felt it. All he had to do was find the damn thing! Finally a sliver of afternoon light glinted on silver, catching his eye. There it was, half hidden underneath a pile of leaves against the base of an old tree. Still without strength, he crawled to the dagger, grabbed the hilt in his bloodied hand, and stood. His vision dimmed, his head swam, but he did not fall. Instead he rested against the tree for a few short seconds, and then he pushed himself away and started walking slowly back toward Arthes, back toward the very place Lyssa had warned him to avoid. He did not return the dagger to its sheath but gripped it in his hand.

Perhaps he was a fool to take on the emperor's army with no other weapon than this, but for now, it would have to suffice.

Lyssa woke in a dark, cold room, lying awkwardly on a stone floor. There were no windows, and she was almost positive that she was underground. She felt as if she were suffocating, as if she were alone and falling endlessly, just as she had in her dreams. Dreams she hadn't had since marrying Blade.

But she was not falling. Nor was she truly alone. She rested her hand on her flat stomach. She'd heard her friends talk about knowing they were with child long before there was any physical indication of their condition. Edine had claimed to know the very night she conceived her first child, and a couple of other friends had told similar tales. Lyssa had never said so, since it would have been rude, but she'd thought those tales to be, well, hooey.

Until she'd been thrown onto a horse and her first thought had been *Don't hurt my baby*. Was it a real knowing or just wishful thinking on her part? Given her current situation, it was possible she would never find out. The baby seemed so real to her. So wonderfully true.

A baby. A part of her, the part that wanted to escape from this harsh reality, wondered when—where—the baby had been conceived. On that first night, in an alleyway? In a soft bed in the home she and Blade had shared for such a short time? On a forest floor, as thoughts of true love teased her?

She could not afford to lose herself in such wonderings. Reality could not be denied for long.

The only light in the room crept around the edges of a door. Her head ached; her entire body was sore. She could not help but groan as she mentally surveyed the soreness. From the top of her head to the tips of her toes, she hurt.

Was Blade dead, or had she been quick enough—and powerful enough—to heal him? She would probably never know. If he did wake and find her gone, he would surely take the opportunity to escape from her and the chaos she had brought to his life. In spite of what he'd said, in spite of the kiss…any sane man would run. With a distance between them the magic would fade away and he would be free to go on without her. At least, she hoped that was true. She wanted him to survive, to live.

"You are awake at last," a man whispered hoarsely. He was in the room with her, too close. Lyssa scurried away from that voice, stood, and placed her back against the wall. Her muscles ached from the struggle and the awkward ride, but fear made her forget the pain for a moment. She heard the snick of a match, watched the flame flare to life, saw it catch the wick of a fat candle. The opposite corner of the small room was lit, illuminating a man in a dark cloak. His face was turned away from her, lost in deep shadow.

"What do you want with me?"

He took a step toward her. She had no place to go, nowhere to run, but she pressed her back more firmly against the wall as if she might be able to move through it if she tried hard enough.

"You should be grateful to me and my men for saving you." When she saw his face she caught her breath and held it. In her mind, she had seen Blade kill this man with a sword. It would probably not be wise to share that information.

Volker.

"Grateful?" She choked on the word. "Your men killed my husband, hit me over the head, and now I am prisoner in this dank, windowless room. *Grateful?*"

"Yes, *grateful*, witch. My girls very much want you dead, but with your husband gone, I don't see how you'll be much of a threat to our plans. I should like the opportunity to study you before I see to your disposal. If you are useful to me, perhaps I will let you live."

Lyssa had been afraid before. First of a witch's prophecy, then of being truly alone. For weeks now she had feared herself, feared what she had become—or was becoming. Then there was her terror of losing Blade—to his need for vengeance and a sword, or to the indifference he had shown her in early days. Loss was loss. But she had never before suffered this kind of fear. This man meant to *study* her. While she did not know exactly what that might entail, she doubted it would be pleasant. And since she had no intention of helping him in any way, she would soon be dead.

All that blood she'd seen in her mind as she'd thought of Arthes…it was hers.

Blade had suffered from fear himself, and now she understood in a way she had not before. He had feared her ability to change him, to take away the pain in his heart. If she could heal him deep inside, could she heal others? Her touch had removed the dark magic that gifted the sentinels who'd killed Blade with unnatural silence. Would a touch shift this man's soul from evil to good? She took a step forward, raising her hand slowly as she approached him. She attempted to harness the power that until now had come and gone with little control on her part. If it was hers, then she should—must—learn control. Just a few steps; that was all it would take to reach him.

"It will not work," Volker said with humor when she was two steps away. "I know what you can do. I've been warned. At least, I have been told what you *should* be able to do. It's all very interesting and a bit unexpected, I must say. With your partner dead, you should be weakened, but even if that is not the case…I understand that you were able to heal your husband's heart in the last days of his life because he still had a little bit of it left. I do not."

And suddenly she was afraid of him in another way. A man with no soul, no heart. If she touched him, would she absorb that horrid darkness instead of offering light? She could heal, she knew that now. Could the same pathways that allowed her to heal also make her vulnerable to evil?

"How do you know so much about me?" she asked. "Are you a wizard?" *A demon? A monster?*

"No. My girls, my lovely demons, they told me all about you. The witch and the blade, one to heal and one to kill. You two are—or rather *were*—a part of their collective consciousness, a shared fear, a shared prophecy. They say that together you could've ruined my plan. Alone you are nothing more than an annoyance."

More. Yes.

His lovely demons…Ksana? The woman Lyssa had sensed on Level Two? Apparently that Ksana had sisters. Of course she did…

Vellance's words came back to Lyssa as clearly as if the old woman stood beside her now. *"Do you think the Isen Demon is the only darkness that blights Columbyana and the lands beyond? There is more darkness than light in this world, girl. The light must fight to remain the stronger of the two."*

Lyssa dropped her hand and took a step back. Again, her back was pressed to the cold wall. Calling upon a gift that had apparently been enhanced by her fear, she once again reached for the magic she had tried to deny. This time that magic came to her much too easily, as if it was and always had been a part of her. She saw the darkness that surrounded the man—Volker, the man Blade had come to Arthes to kill—as if it were a tangible thing. There was not a drop of light, not a glimmer of hope, in or around him. She absolutely must *not* touch him.

Shaking, she returned to her corner, bowed her head, and closed her eyes. Volker chuckled, and it was a frightful sound. No doubt he thought she was praying fruitlessly to the gods and goddesses, or to the One God, but she was not.

Blade had found her in the forest when he should not have been able to. The thick woods were vast and not easy to navigate, and yet he had located her as if he'd known all along where she would be. If she had healed him, if he lived, could she reach for him as he had reached for her? Could she touch him in spite of the physical distance between them?

And if she could reach him, what would she say? Should she beg Blade to save her, or tell him to run in the other direction, far and fast?

It didn't matter. She tried, but there was nothing. As strong and real as her newfound magic had felt moments earlier, as much a part of her as it had become…maybe it had not been enough this time. Maybe her powerful and otherworldly connection with Blade was gone because he was gone. Tears slipped down her face, and she felt a new despair.

Just as Vellance had predicted, she was alone. And just as in her worse nightmares, she was lost in the dark.

Lyssa had saved him, of that he had no doubt, but Blade could not call himself fully healed. He was weak, and there was still a lot of pain in his chest. What if Lyssa had only healed his skin and beneath…beneath he was ripped to shreds?

No, the pain was lessening as he walked, not getting worse.

As he had found her before, he would find her again. The feeling pulling him back toward Arthes was more powerful than ever before, as if a long silken thread connected him to Lyssa and was reeling him back to the city. If the attackers had left horses waiting nearby, it was likely she was already there, but in whose hands?

He didn't know, but he would find her.

As he walked he thought of Lyssa, and of Runa. Normally thoughts of Runa were so painful that he turned to drink or violence to push her memory away. But this time, after actually seeing her again—however briefly, through fever dream or a visit to the Land of the Dead—he did not crave whisky or a good fistfight.

He was capable of love; he was not entirely broken.

Blade tried not to think of Runa's words about a daughter. A daughter that was, or a daughter that would be? A real visitation and message from the dead, or a wish?

Or a fear.

No matter, the thought of a child was a distraction, and at this moment he needed to focus only on his wife. If he found Lyssa, if he saved her…he would never again deny her. He would share her bed every night, if she would have him. If she wasn't already with child, she soon enough would be.

But first he had to save her, and he had no idea from who, or what.

Not far from Arthes, the man who had used the name Stasio for the past six years changed course. Instead of heading west toward Tryfyn he turned to the north. His time in Arthes was finished, for now. He was needed in the mountains, where others of his kind had gathered.

When he could see the mountains of the north in the distance, snow-topped even though spring had arrived and illuminated by moonlight, he dismounted and removed the long robe he'd worn for the six years he had served that fool Miron Volker. The robe had served his purpose. While someone might send out a search party for the wizard Stasio, they would have a hard time coming up with any description other than the long, black, hooded robe.

The robe was enchanted. Some would remember him as being tall. Others would insist he was short. Some would say Stasio was a young man; others would argue that he was old. A few might remember a limp. None would remember his face.

The girl walked toward him, coming from the north to meet him. Though the night was cool, her arms and feet were bare. Long pale hair caught the moonlight, as did her plain silvery dress. He had been expecting her.

Guiding his horse by the reins, he walked toward her. There was no need to hurry. When she was close enough to hear him, he said.

"Linara, yes?"

"Yes," she replied.

Linara was not the name this beautiful creature had been given at birth. Before her mother had died she'd named her child for a beautiful and poisonous flower. Ksana. This woman child was the first of the Ksana demons, the most powerful. Moonlight lit her face. She was by far the most beautiful of a species of unbearably beautiful girls.

He had not met her, not in person, but they had communicated in a way only the most powerful among them could. Across a great distance, with words and with emotion, in dreams and in quiet moments, they had come to know one another well.

"I am here," she said simply.

"As I see." This night, this meeting, had been planned for the past two years. The day, the place, the hour. "Did you kill the woman who dared to falsely call herself your mother?"

Linara smiled, and his heart—which was small and hard and had never known love—hitched in his chest. Such a smile could bring down emperors. "Of course not. Kill a Fyne witch and you bring down the wrath of a powerful clan you do not wish to face."

"You ran away?" he asked. "How very…ordinary."

"I told my mother…Sophie…that I had to get away, that I needed to be alone for a while. She didn't like it, she tried to talk me out of leaving, but she understood. Too many people know my secret."

When they met on the road they both stopped walking. He reached out and cupped her cheek in one hand. "We have much to do, Linara."

"Yes, I know. And I am ready."

"One born, one hatched, one created...they were talked of in hushed whispers among wizards long before the first of your kind was born. Those three will stop us, if we don't stop them first."

"That's why I'm here...Stasio? Should I call you Stasio?"

She turned about and they walked side by side toward the mountains. Far in the distance, visible only to one whose vision was extraordinary, a speck of dragon's fire lit the sky.

"For now, that name will do."

Chapter Fifteen

Lyssa slept fitfully on a cold stone floor, without a blanket or a pillow. Her supper had been a piece of hard bread. There had not been enough light to see if there was mold on the bread or not, but she had eaten it anyway. She was starving. She had to eat, for the baby if not for herself. For a few terrible moments she had wondered if there really was a baby, if the idea of a child—Blade's child—was anything more than a fantasy, a wish.

No, the baby was real. She had come to accept that; to embrace it.

By her reckoning it had been a full day since she'd lost Blade. The hours moved too slowly here, but she could not allow her fear to cause her to become so disoriented that she lost all track of time. She ate, she slept, and she did her best to keep her wits about her.

She dreamed not of Volker or of being trapped in a cold room of stone, but of Blade. In her dream he came toward her. Sometimes he ran, but often he could not. There were times when he could barely walk. He was too tired, too badly hurt. She saw him steal a horse, saw him race toward Arthes and her, and she heard him call her name. Sometimes in a whisper, sometimes with a shout, as if her name were a war cry. Again and again, she heard him call her name.

The baby was real, but dreams of Blade—alive and coming for her—were nothing more than fantasy. As much as she wished them to be real…

She woke when the door to her cell opened with a screech and a clang. Naturally it was Volker, the man who had killed Blade's sister, the man who collected demon children. Fifteen and sixteen years old, they were no longer true children. They were young women who wished her dead. Lyssa sat up and scooted back, away from the man.

Volker carried with him a steaming mug of something. Tea, broth, chocolate…whatever it was, the sight of that mug made her mouth water. On second thought, if he was bringing her anything it was probably drugged. Poisoned. Did she dare eat anything that came from his hands? Heaven help her, what choice did she have?

He offered her the mug, but she hugged her arms to herself and shook her head.

After a disgusted snort, he took a sip from the heavy mug and then passed it to her again. This time she grabbed the mug, took a sip herself, and closed her eyes in something near joy. Or relief. She drank again. Tea with milk and plenty of honey poured down her throat, and it tasted good.

"I don't plan to kill you just yet, witch," he said harshly. "I wish to know more before I make that decision. And as I said, if you prove useful to me I might allow you to live."

She did not respond. His idea of living and hers were likely worlds apart. Lyssa had no desire to be one of his girls; she would not assist the man who had murdered Blade's sister—the man who had ordered Blade killed—in any way.

"Are you often ill, Lyssa?" he asked in a calm, almost caring voice.

She cupped the mug in both hands. It was warm, a comfort in this chilled room. Her next sip was a small one, as she savored the tea. She would take whatever small comforts she could, while she could. "No. I have always been very healthy."

"Of course you have," he whispered. "Not a fever, not a cough, not a stomachache."

"No."

"May I see your hand, Lyssa?"

She saw no reason not to comply, since he could, if he wished, wrestle with her or hit her over the head to get what he wanted. Grudgingly, she shifted the mug of tea to one hand and offered him the other, palm up.

There was little light in the room, so by the time she saw the glint of steel in his hand it was too late. He swiped the dagger across her palm, and it cut deep. She dropped the mug. It crashed to the stone floor, breaking into many small pieces. Warm tea spread across the floor, wasted.

Perhaps Lyssa was unusually healthy, but she could feel pain, and she did bleed.

By the time Blade rode into Arthes on a stolen horse, the pain of his wounds was almost gone. One full day since he'd been wounded to the brink of death—and perhaps beyond—and he was healed.

Lyssa was in the palace, he knew. He *felt*. She was hidden deep, in terrible danger, and scared. He kept a sharp eye out for sentinels who might recognize him, but those few he passed on his way to Cyrus's shop paid him no more mind than they would any other traveler on horseback. Mud on his clothing disguised most of the blood, so his appearance did not draw their attention. A quick glance would reveal nothing but another dirty traveler. Only on closer inspection was the dried blood noticeable.

It took a great deal of self-control not to confront those sentinels he passed. Had the attackers who'd taken Lyssa been true sentinels or thieves in stolen uniforms? No matter. To make his move too soon would be foolish, and would not lead him to his wife.

His heart was pounding as he hitched the horse to a post outside the shop. It was near closing time. The afternoon sun hung low in the sky, and on the street Arthes residents walked and rode toward home. Children laughed. Women chattered.

Blade's mission had been altered, but in some ways, nothing had changed. If he rushed into the palace, he would be killed long before he got to Lyssa. He was willing to risk his own life, but he would not risk hers. And he could not be stopped before he found her.

Cyrus was at the counter, waiting on a customer, smiling as if all was right with the world. He could not know what had happened, but he had to know that Lyssa and her new husband were missing. Most likely he had also heard the accusation of witchcraft from Edine or someone the silly nit had spoken to. He had no right to smile.

That smile died quickly when Cyrus looked up and saw Blade. He paled and stepped back, looking for a moment as if he might actually run.

Blade stalked to the counter, glared down at the lone customer, an elderly man with a love for sweets, and said, "Out."

The man didn't hesitate to leave, abandoning his purchases on the counter and taking his coins with him.

"Where is Lyssa?" Cyrus asked, unexpectedly taking the offensive. "What have you done with her?"

"Do you care?" Blade snapped. "Don't lie to me."

"I do, I do care, but—" He pointed a shaking finger to Blade's chest. "Dear God, is that her blood? Did you harm her? I know she's different, she's not like the rest of us, but she deserves…I wanted better for her than…"

"The blood is my own." Suddenly the occasional odd glances made sense. The shifting of Cyrus's eyes, the infrequent flashes of…fear. "You know what she is, don't you? All along, you knew, and yet you didn't warn her, didn't prepare her for this."

"I don't know what you're talking about." Cyrus's face went red with his lie, then paled again. His eyes darted to the side and then back to Blade.

"You know very well," Blade said in a low voice. "It's the reason you were so relieved when she married me. It's the reason you were so anxious to have her out of your house. You were afraid of her, afraid of what she might become."

Cyrus sighed. Two spots of color rose on his cheeks. "Lyssa's mother was a witch. I didn't know when I married her, didn't know until she became pregnant. That's when her abilities came to the surface. It was not bad, at first, but then…she began to lose control. One day she picked Lyssa up and the baby screamed. Her flesh, where Madra had touched her, was burned. She healed quickly, but after that Madra was afraid to touch her own child. A week later she disappeared."

"Lyssa's mother isn't dead?"

"I don't know. It's been many years, and she was…Madra was not well when she left us. And yes, I have always been afraid that what happened to Madra would happen to my daughter. I was not afraid of Lyssa. I was afraid *for* her."

Maybe that was, in part, true. Blade didn't have time to dig any deeper now. He had no time to waste…not a moment.

"Lyssa is in danger. If you ever loved her, if you care for her at all, you will help me."

"What…what do you need?" He again studied Blade's ripped and muddied and bloodied clothing. "Other than a change of clothes."

"I need a sword."

Cyrus shook his head. "I have none, but I can take you to a blacksmith…"

"There's no time for that." No time at all. "Get me into the palace," Blade said. "Now."

Lyssa was lying on the floor of her cell again. It had become impossible to sit, much less stand. The stone was grimy and cold, but she pressed her cheek to it. She could wish for blessed sleep and nightmares of being alone, but they did not come. There was only pain, weakness, and despair. So many nights, so many years wasted fearing solitude, when there were monsters in the world far more worthy of fear.

"Fascinating," Volker said. He'd lit several candles for this visit, so she could see him better than before. That was unfortunate, since he was the person she most wished never to see again. His face might be considered ordinary, if one did not note the gleam of sick hate in his eyes. He enjoyed hurting her; he enjoyed her screams.

She had long ago ceased begging him to stop, since pleading only made him smile. Again he took his dagger to her flesh, to her arm, for the third or fourth or fifth time. It hurt, she bled, and then the wound healed, her skin knitting itself closed. But not until she'd lost blood. She'd lost too much blood in too short a period of time, and that was why she could no longer sit up. What was this torture doing to her child, her baby, Blade's daughter?

Blade's daughter. If her mind was not playing tricks on her, their baby was a girl. Would she be a witch like her mother? Would the child even be born into this world? For that to happen, Lyssa had to survive.

She would have pleaded for her child, would have begged for the life of her baby, if she hadn't thought Volker would be thrilled to use the child against her. There were moments when he seemed to know what she was thinking, but he did not know everything. He could not know about the baby.

No, he did not hear her thoughts; he had no access to her mind. He got his information from someone else. One of the half-demons, or a wizard, or a witch whose circumstances were no better than Lyssa's. Volker had no magic of his own, but he was truly evil.

As she opened her eyes and watched, Volker took one of the vials he'd filled with her blood and drank it. He smacked his thin lips, licked away a drop of blood that had clung to the corner of his mouth and dribbled down into his beard. "It doesn't taste any different from a normal woman's blood."

The fact that he knew what a normal woman's blood tasted like raised the level of her horror.

She was barely able to move by the time he placed the tip of the dagger at her throat. "If I cut off your head, will it grow back? You can't be immune to every illness or injury. You must have *some* vulnerability." He moved the tip of the knife down her body until it rested over her belly. "What if I cut the child from your body? There's not much to her yet, is there? Does your daughter already have a heart? Is that tiny creature filled with powerful blood like yours?"

How did he know? Maybe he had known all along, thanks to his girls. Maybe he had known before she had...

"I am not with child." Lyssa found the strength to reach out and grab his wrist as she lied. She did not like to touch him, but she had to move that dagger away from her baby. Sadly, she did not have the strength to control him. After pushing that hand away, it returned. Stronger, more threatening.

"Don't lie to me, witch. My girls see everything, they know everything. And they tell me what they see...what they know."

"Do you have no powers of your own?" she countered, knowing that he didn't, knowing also that he believed his lack of magic to be a weakness. Judging by the expression on his face, it had been the wrong thing to say. He could—would—kill her.

Would Blade be waiting for her on the other side? Would the Land of the Dead be as real as this world? She wanted to hold him again, to tell him how much she loved him. They should be together. In any world, they could be *more*...

The tip of Volker's dagger raised up, danced about, and finally raked across her forearm. He increased the pressure, and once again, she bled.

Blade moved unerringly forward, drawn toward Lyssa just as he had been when he'd followed her into the forest. The guards were lulled by Cyrus's presence. They were accustomed to seeing the shopkeeper come and go. The bolt of fabric the old man carried gave them an excuse for entering.

Once inside, Cyrus was taken to the empress. Blade followed his instincts and slipped away. A door just off the central ground floor room called to him, and he answered without hesitation. He opened the door, followed the narrow steps down. Beneath the earth, into what had once been a prison level but was now deserted—or should be—he answered.

The palace was rumored to have many hidden passageways and secret rooms. What if Lyssa was in one of them? What if he could feel her so near and yet not find her?

Doubts were pushed away. He *would* find her. He had not cheated death and come all this way to leave without his wife.

Lyssa closed her eyes and felt the blood seep from her body. She was going to die. Here, soon. No amount of magic could save her from this.

And then, when it seemed that the last bit of hope had left her, her eyes popped open. The dark, terrible room seemed to fill with sunshine. Her heart thudded, strong once more. Much as she had felt blood seeping from her body, she now felt life seeping in. Blade was near. Very near. He wasn't dead; he was very much alive. He was coming for her, coming for her and their baby.

"I do not like this new expression on your face, witch," Volker said. Moving fluidly he stood and stepped away from her, and then he was gone. He closed the door to her cell behind him, but he was in such a hurry he did not even take the time to lock it. As if she could move...as if she had the strength to save herself.

In a matter of moments the door opened again. Lyssa opened her eyes, stared in fear at the shadow that filled the doorway. And then she relaxed; her body almost sang. She could not see his face nearly well enough, but she would know that shape, that body, anywhere.

"Blade." The single word was a sigh, a prayer of gratitude, a declaration of love. And then she closed her eyes and allowed the blessed darkness to overtake her.

Chapter Sixteen

Blade stood over Lyssa for several moments before he dared to drop to his haunches and touch her. There was so much blood. It was in her hair, soaked into her dress; it stained every visible inch of her skin.

She breathed. He placed two fingers at her slender throat. The pulse there was fast, and not as strong as he would like.

But she was alive; he was not too late.

This lower level, which had once been used as an underground prison, before the emperor had moved the guardhouse and cells to another site well away from the palace, had been deserted when he'd burst into the hallway. He could not expect that good luck would last for long. If Volker used these cells, he or others in his employ might be nearby. He scooped Lyssa into his arms and carried her into the hallway. There was no way to go but the way he'd come in, up narrow stairs to ground level. He'd walked into the palace with Cyrus, who had a plausible reason for entry. Getting out of the palace with a blood-soaked woman in his arms would not be as easy as getting in had been, however.

Sure enough, as he burst from the stairway with Lyssa in his arms, several pairs of curious eyes turned his way. Two sentinels drew their swords.

Blade could not draw his dagger, not unless he put Lyssa down, and he would not do that. The floor would be too hard and cold; she needed him, needed him to hold her.

Fortunately the sentinels looked more confused than alarmed. They'd seen him come in with Cyrus, and they knew Lyssa well. She'd been visiting this palace with her father since she was a child.

"My wife…my wife fell down the stairs, and she's hurt herself badly." The fear in his voice was real, so real the words came out rougher than he'd intended. "I must get her home. Our family physician will care for her there."

One of the sentinels took a step forward. "Gods, that's a lot of blood. Are you sure she's alive?"

At that moment Empress Morgana herself entered the room. Blade had only seen the emperor's wife from a distance, but it was her. The fair-haired empress was elegantly beautiful, elaborately dressed, and had an air of command. Cyrus was right behind the empress, still trying—ineptly—to explain away his mistake in delivering a length of fabric that had not been ordered. The empress came to a sudden stop, and her smile faded as she looked from the sentinels to Lyssa and then caught Blade's eye. She was clearly alarmed and yet still very much in control.

Cyrus glanced at his daughter, and his face lost all color. Blade had made it clear that Lyssa was in grave danger, but her father had not expected to see her this way. "Oh, Lyssa," he whispered, with love and fear combined, as he dropped the length of fabric to the floor.

Morgana took charge. It was an empress's way, Blade imagined.

"She fell, you say?"

Blade did his best to bow with the unconscious Lyssa in his arms. "My apologies, Your Highness. My wife allowed her curiosity to overcome her, and she poked her nose where it did not belong. She fell down the stairs and cut her head. You know how head wounds bleed. I am hoping it looks much worse than it is."

"Miss Lyssa was not with her husband and father when they arrived," one confused sentinel offered.

"Of course she was," Blade said. Her father concurred, though not as vigorously as he might have. Two against one. Was it enough?

Morgana turned an icy glare to the offending sentinel. "Fetch the palace physician and see that a guest room on Level Seven is prepared."

Blade stepped forward; Lyssa stirred in his arms. Thank God! "That's not necessary. I can care for my wife. As I said, it—"

The empress turned the same cold glare she'd sent the sentinel's way to Blade, cutting him off. "I will not allow her to leave the palace this way. What will people think if they see Lyssa leaving here bloodied and unconscious?" Then she smiled. That smile was a mixture of beauty and the power Columbyana's empress possessed. He had heard tales of her magical abilities, but had no idea what was true and what was mere speculation.

"I am sure that she will be fine," the empress said. "She is strong, her heartbeat is…becoming steady. I must offer a room for her to rest, at the very least. You can attempt to care for her yourself if you wish, but the physician will be close by."

It was not a request but an order. One he dare not refuse.

While Blade did not know the full extent of Empress Morgana's powers, he was relieved to hear her say that Lyssa's heartbeat was becoming steadier. "You are too kind."

Cyrus was dismissed, while Blade—Lyssa in his arms—was guided by the empress herself up three flights of winding stairs to a long hallway and, eventually, a luxurious bed chamber. The empress ordered a hot bath, hot soup, and clean clothing to be provided, as well as bandages, soap, and her own special salve.

"You will stay the night, of course," she said, as she indicated the physician, who was already on standby in the hallway.

"Of course," Blade responded, trying not to sound upset. Was that truly a physician just beyond the door, or was the nondescript man a guard?

Morgana met his gaze. "I consider Lyssa a friend. If anyone tries to hurt her, they will have me to contend with." It was a very definite threat. "She's not going anywhere until I know she's well. And safe."

Did the empress think Blade himself had hurt her? Did she believe that he would? Or could? He answered her with a bow and a nod and then she was gone.

All his hard work to get into the palace and here he was, trapped and desperate to get Lyssa *out*.

Lyssa roused to warmth, softness, and a loving touch. Blade's whispers pierced the blessed darkness that had claimed her, and in response she felt herself grow stronger.

Her eyes fluttered open. Blade smiled down at her, though that smile, illuminated by candlelight, was weak.

"You found me," she whispered.

"Again," he added.

"You should have run away, you should have gone to the sea without me…"

"Never."

With a gasp, she tried to sit up. Blade held her down, gently. "Volker," she said, her voice weak. "He…did you see him? Did you pass him in the hallway?"

Blade shook his head. "I did not see him."

"If I didn't pass out between the time Volker left the cell and you entered, and I don't think I did, then…"

"Don't worry about that now. Either you did lose consciousness or he had another way to exit that level. Secret passageways, hidden rooms. I don't know and I don't care." His voice was rough.

"Where are we?" A quick glance told her that they were not in any place she had ever been before. The room was large and finely furnished, and decorated in gold and varying shades of blue. There was a collection of delicately crafted colored glass on a long table against one wall, blue and green and lavender, that caught the light and sparkled.

"In the palace, Level Seven," Blade said. "The empress insisted."

She realized that Blade had cut away her ruined frock and had been in the process of bathing her with a wet cloth when she awoke. She remained sticky with blood and was glad that there was no mirror nearby. The sight of her face as she knew it must look now would have given her nightmares for the rest of her life, she imagined. It was bad enough to see the blood and dirt on her legs and arms.

Steam rose from an ornate tub, not far from the side of the bed.

"Help me into that bath," she said, and Blade wrapped his arms around her and helped her to sit up, swing her legs over the side of the bed and stand. Though she was weaker than she would have liked, she was stronger than she should have been. She thought of Volker and his knife, and clung to Blade's arm as he helped her to the tub.

She stepped into the hot water, sank down, and leaned her head against the back of the tub, sighing in delight. The water was so wonderfully hot it could not have been waiting for her very long. Nothing had ever felt better. Well, *almost* nothing. "Hold my hand?" She lifted her left hand above the water, and Blade took it. Squeezed. Held on tight.

"You have truly ruined me, you know," he said, his voice low.

"In what way?"

"Revenge is no longer all I desire. You make me want more. You make me want everything."

She smiled. "Are you sorry?"

He hesitated before answering. "I haven't decided."

She remembered what Volker had said and wondered if the horrible man had realized at the time that he was offering her much needed information. He'd never meant for her to leave that dark cell, had perhaps not even meant for her to survive the night. But she had. "I could not have healed you inside if there had not been a heart to heal. If your soul had truly been beyond saving, no amount of magic would have been sufficient to pull you back from the brink of darkness. I have not changed you as much as you think. I only uncovered what was already there."

He didn't respond except to take a clean cloth, wet it and begin to wash her face. His touch was gentle, easy and loving. Though she could not see, she could feel the dried blood being wiped away. Even after the blood was gone, Blade continued to wash her. He obviously liked touching her, and she liked being touched.

Finally she dipped her head beneath the water, wet her hair and allowed Blade to wash it for her. As he massaged her scalp and washed the blood away, she closed her eyes and allowed herself to experience the pleasure his touch roused in her.

She almost told him what she suspected—no, what she knew to be true. They were having a baby. But not here, and not like this. The time would come, though, and soon. Would he be happy or terrified?

She would share the news as they sat before a fire in their own home, whether that home was Hagan's cottage or a shack elsewhere. She would take Blade's hand, look into his eyes and tell him, "We're going to have a baby." Whether he was happy or horrified, she would kiss him and make it all better. It was her place to do just that.

She was no longer angry with her father and Sinmora for not telling her about their own baby. The time for the sharing of such news needed to be…right.

When she stepped from the tub, the water she left behind was pink and soapy, but she was clean once more. And stronger than she'd been when she'd stepped into her bath. Blade took a large thick towel and dried her body. Slowly, with gentle hands and a loving touch. How someone so large could be so gentle, she could not imagine. When her body was dry he rubbed the towel in her hair until it was no longer dripping wet. She sat on the side of the bed, and he reached for a dress that was laid out on a massive wing chair. It was not her dress, she had never seen it before, but she recognized the fabric. It was a lovely shade of gold; it shimmered in the light. She never wore such bright colors. Wearing that dress she would not be able to blend into the crowd. People would look at her. They would stare. *Bad Luck Lyssa. Witch.*

"Not yet," she said, and Blade dropped the fine dress and turned to her. "Comb my hair?"

He sat beside her on the bed and did as she asked, gently combing the knots away, one narrow strand at a time. By the time he was done her hair was almost dry. It fell over her shoulders, damp and waving, when he set the comb aside.

"Make love to me?"

The question surprised him. "But you were…"

"When we're together, when we're connected, I grow stronger. Nothing will make me heal faster than making love to you." And it was more than healing, she knew that now. She and Blade were incomplete alone, but together…together they fit like two pieces of those intricate wooden puzzles her father sometimes sold in his shop.

Blade placed a hand, large and warm, beneath her belly button. Lyssa held her breath? Did he know about the baby? Did he somehow just *know*, the same way she did? But his hand didn't linger there. It moved lower, slowly, surely. He spread her thighs and stroked her where she was already wet for him.

"I should have known you would find me."

"Yes, you should have," he whispered as he kissed the side of her neck. For a few wonderful moments she relaxed in his arms and let him arouse her. Not that she'd needed much in the way of arousing. Neither did he, she noted when she reached out to caress him.

"I once wondered how you managed to walk down the street with this hard length between your legs. I understand now that it isn't always so, but I still find it…fascinating."

She removed his shirt, taking her time, running her hands over his chest and arms as they were revealed to her. He was so hard all over. Once he had been hard inside and out, but now…now he knew love. Amazingly, impossibly, he loved her. Would it last? Was it real? Those were questions for another time. Right now, at this moment, it was real enough.

He stood by the side of the bed to shuck off his boots and pants, and then he was in bed beside her. She loved the feel of his bare skin against hers, loved the image of her pale skin pressing against his tanned flesh. He spread her legs and teased her again, his fingers dancing around and then inside her.

"From a dark alley at midnight to a room in the imperial palace," she whispered in his ear. "We have come far in a short period of time, love."

Blade rolled her onto her back, and then he was inside her. With every stroke, pleasure and power grew. Soon it didn't matter if they were in an alley or a palace. All that mattered was the strength of their bonding, the pleasure they brought to one another. The love. The love was most important of all.

Any lingering pain she might have suffered faded. With love and pleasure, Blade wiped the nightmare that was Miron Volker from her mind. How had she lived without this? Without *him*?

And then there were just the two of them and the way their bodies fit together. Pleasure grew. It teased her; it enveloped her.

Lyssa climaxed and screamed, not caring who might hear. Release whipped through her body, as if a thousand golden threads pulled and danced inside her. She felt Blade's release, savored it as she had savored her own.

He collapsed atop her, cradled her in his hot arms. "I do love you, you know," she whispered.

He did not respond, and she was not terribly surprised. Love had not been in his plans; it was likely more of an annoyance to him than it was to her. But she was hurt. A little. She shouldn't be, she should understand, but the heart wasn't always practical. The heart didn't respond to reason.

Maybe, like her, Blade wondered what was real and what was magic.

Chapter Seventeen

Princess stood at the open window and howled. Father had ignored her requests for an audience for *hours*, and now it was too late. The witch and the blade were here, and there would be no stopping them now.

She turned to face her sisters. "We do not need Minister Volker to take what is rightfully ours." She would not call him Father, not ever again. "He's delayed too long, and now our enemies are stronger than ever." That was all the explanation that was necessary. Her sisters knew what she knew; they shared thoughts, knowledge, fears.

Princess stared at Runa, but only for a moment. That one could hide too much, she kept her own secrets. It was alarming, it was a worry, but for now they needed one another. They had no one else.

"How can we escape?" Runa asked, too meekly for one so powerful. "We are too far off the ground to leave by the window, and the door is only opened once every three or four days for feeding."

Princess was tired of sharing nourishment with two others. The power she took in was insufficient. Volker was probably keeping them weak on purpose. Was he afraid? He should be.

She wanted to be fed well and often. Otherwise, how would she reach her full power and become the leader she was meant to be?

"We're due for a meal, are we not?" Princess looked at Runa, who was outwardly the weakest of the three of them, the quiet one, the one least likely to be seen as a threat. It was embarrassing, that a Ksana could be so timid. "Tell the sentinels that you're starving and in need of immediate nourishment." After the death of one of their own, they would not even speak to Princess through a closed door, much less open it to her. "Tell them Divya and I are asleep, but you cannot sleep because your hunger is too great." She smiled. "Tell them last time I refused to share." They would believe that.

But Runa didn't move toward the door. She was uncertain still.

Princess looked to Divya and sent a silent communication. Without further prodding, the more obedient sister moved to the closed door. In a deceptively sweet voice, she crooned, "When will we feed again?" Then, in an exaggerated whisper, she added, "Princess will not share, and I am so very hungry." When no one answered, she said, "Father will be displeased if I die from hunger."

After a short pause a male voice responded, "I will see to it."

"Soon," Divya said, her voice almost pathetic as she gave Princess a wicked smile.

Runa said, "You're going to kill him, aren't you?"

"How else can we expect to escape?" Princess argued. "We've been replaced as Volker's favorites, you do realize that, don't you? Can't you feel the others, so near? A shifter, a seer who whispers in his ear, a fire-starter. They are not as strong as us. They are more...malleable. More obedient. Ksanas are not easy to kill, but the man who dared to call himself our Father is searching for a way to do that right now. He brought the witch and the blade into the palace. Beneath our very feet, they grow stronger. I warned him. I told him what had to be done, but did he listen to me? No. He does not deserve our loyalty." She would kill Volker herself, if she could, but he was wary of her and always kept his distance. The best immediate solution was escape. "Our time will come, Runa. You can be a part of the coming revolution, or you can die with the rest of those who oppose us."

Emotions warred on Runa's face. "I don't want to die."

She also didn't want to kill, and that was the problem.

Long hours passed before the sentinel returned. Runa sat upon her bed, unnaturally still the entire time. Divya sang, repeating over and over a pretty tune of a love she would never know. Love was not for their kind. Princess did not make that argument with her; for the moment Divya was happy, dreaming of freedom and what tomorrow might bring. Why should she rob her of that joy?

Princess looked onto the street below, using her increasing powers to reach beyond this palace to others of her kind. Once she escaped, she would find them. Not for the first time, she wished that she had made that escape days ago.

As the night grew long, she began to think their ruse was a complete failure. Escape would come, but not tonight. And then the sentinel at the door whispered, "Are you still there?"

Divya danced to the door on bare feet. "Yes." Her voice was soft, seductive. "Step back," the sentinel said. "I have a beggar for you."

Divya did step back, but not far. Princess stood to the side as the door cracked open. A very confused and very drunken man in rags was thrown into the room, but before the sentinel could close and lock the door, Princess reached out and grabbed his arm. Her slender fingers gripped tightly. She yanked him into the room and threw him to the floor before he could shout and raise an alarm. As he hit the ground the breath left him so he was incapable of calling for help, not that anyone was close enough to hear, and then Princess was on top of him.

She caught his gaze and held it. He was a large man, but he was mentally weak, and that glance alone was enough to capture him. This sentinel was not much older than she. He might be seventeen or eighteen. He had smooth skin, a slender body, long, fine brown hair that might have a touch of red by sunlight. She would never know.

She kissed him. In seconds his life force began to fill her, leaving his body in a fine green mist and moving into her. Mouth, throat, lungs…then that force was everywhere.

"My turn, before he's empty." Divya slapped Princess on the side of the head to get her attention. "The beggar did not have much to give."

Princess slowly, reluctantly, moved away. Soon she would not have to share, but for now she would do what had to be done. She needed her sisters; there was strength in numbers.

Runa stood by the window, her arms wrapped around herself as if she were a child. Princess reached for her thoughts, but saw nothing. The thoughts were there, but they were blocked. Hidden away.

"Aren't you hungry?" Princess asked as Divya finished off the sentinel.

"Always," Runa admitted.

"You need never go hungry." Princess saw the struggle in this one, the fight between dark and light…the uncertainty. Humans had all but ruined Runa, and it would be tempting to try to kill her before she became a liability. Two things stopped her. One, she was not entirely sure how to kill one of their kind. And two, Runa was powerful, more powerful than she let on. She would be an asset to the revolution once she accepted who and what she was.

"Come with us," Princess said as an energized Divya stood. "If you stay behind, Volker will surely kill you."

Runa nodded and followed them to the open door, and together the three of them, sisters now and always, ran for the staircase that would take them down and out, and into a world that was not prepared for the likes of the Ksanas.

Blade dressed slowly. It would be wonderful to stay in bed, to sleep with Lyssa in his arms and forget everything that had brought them to this point. Everything. Even Volker. For the first time in four years, he had a goal that went beyond revenge, a purpose steeped in something other than hate.

He would protect Lyssa with his life, if need be. He would be her defender, the father of her child, her lover…her husband.

"We have to get out of here, Lyssa."

She sighed, rolled toward him. Naked, beautiful, soft, and filled with a magic he did not yet understand. Yes, he was tempted to have her again. And again.

"Why?" she whispered.

"It isn't safe here." He knew it, in his recently healed heart. Sentinels—or mercenaries like those who had taken Runa four years ago—working at Volker's command had kidnapped her, and then the bastard had tortured her under the very noses of those who should have protected her. How many sentinels answered to Volker rather than the emperor? How many palace residents might be spying for the man who'd murdered Runa and hurt Lyssa? Blade didn't know who he could trust, other than his wife, and the empress herself.

"Fine." She rolled from the bed and donned the gold dress. It was not as simply made as her usual gowns, and even he could tell that the fabric was an expensive one. He almost snorted as that thought passed through his head. When had he ever been one to note how expensive a fabric might be? His time in Cyrus's store had not been entirely wasted.

Perhaps when all this was behind him he could be a real shopkeeper instead of playing at being one. With Lyssa beside him, of course. It was an oddly tempting—and temporary—thought. He had never been meant for the life of a shopkeeper. Neither had Lyssa.

"Since you bled on my shirt, this was delivered for me." He held the blue jacket up by one finger and a white shirt by another.

"Fancy," Lyssa said with a wicked grin. "I'm sure you'll be quite pretty in your new outfit."

"Pretty?" He scowled, for effect.

"Well, I do prefer you naked, but that isn't always practical."

"Do you want to get out of here before morning?"

"Of course."

"Then don't say the word 'naked' again."

She laughed. They both dressed quickly, and Lyssa pulled her hair back, using a clip that had been left on the dresser. "I'll return it later," she said. "I can't make an effective escape with my hair falling into my eyes, now can I?"

They shared the soup because they needed the nourishment. He had not known how hungry he was until the now-cold liquid hit his tongue. Lyssa, after her trials, would need more food soon, but for now the soup would suffice.

Blade stuck the dagger into the sheath at his belt, wishing for a sword, certain that he needed that sword as surely as he needed breath.

Lyssa had asked him once if Blade was his real name or a nickname. He hadn't answered, and she hadn't asked again. As he longed for a sword, he remembered his mother's words from long ago. *I had planned to name you after my brother, but the night before you were born I dreamed of a great, gleaming sword. It was beautiful, and the blade shone with an unnatural light. It twisted and twirled, catching the light and singing in the air. So beautiful. I thought that dream to be a sign, and so I named you Blade.*

He'd always believed his mother's dream to be nothing more than that, a dream—until now.

Blade opened the door and looked into the hallway. The only person he could see from his position was the physician, who was dozing in a chair against the opposite wall. The man opened one eye, alerted by the movement of the heavy door, and sat up straight when he saw Blade standing there.

"Has Miss Lyssa taken a turn for the worse? The empress is quite concerned about her well-being."

"No," Blade said calmly. "She's much better, in fact. I know it's rather late, but she's hungry. Could you perhaps fetch a bite from the kitchen? The soup is long gone, I'm afraid. We would much appreciate it." There had been a time when he would have disposed of the physician in a more direct manner, not by killing him, if it could be avoided, but with a knock on the head and a length of rope. But the man was innocent and did not deserve to be attacked if there was any way around it.

The physician stood, stretched his limbs and nodded. "I could use a bite of something myself. I'll be back as soon as possible."

"No rush," Blade said.

The physician walked crisply down the hallway and turned toward the stairwell. Blade waited a moment or two, and then he reached back for Lyssa's hand. She took it and held on.

The palace was so quiet at night. Most of the residents slept, he supposed, though sentinels would be on guard, particularly on the lower floors where the emperor and his family slept. The hallway wasn't dark as he had thought it might be, but was dimly illuminated by the occasional flickering candle. Sconces were set into the stone walls at regular intervals, and some of them were lit. Others were dark. He grabbed a candle as he passed an ornate table, in case the stairwell was not as bright as the corridor.

"Where will we go?" Lyssa whispered as they reached the end of the long hall.

He released her hand, gave her the candle, and drew his dagger. He did not know what he might find around each corner, and there were many corners and twists in the imperial palace.

"We'll decide that once we're out." Hagan would help, if asked, as would Lyssa's father. But those were the first places anyone looking for them would go. He kissed her, too quickly, and shielded her with his body as they rounded the corner. The hallway was blessedly clear.

With silent steps they entered the stairwell. There was a hint of light, as if candles burned at intervals along the way. Just below them an unexpected sound echoed up the twisting stairway. He could have sworn it was a girlish giggle.

♦ ♦ ♦

Lyssa trusted Blade with her heart and with her life. She had never trusted anyone so much, she knew that now. Not a potential husband, not her stepmother, not Edine, not even her father. She would put her life into Blade's hands any day.

She was doing so at this moment.

Lyssa was aware in a way she had never been before, as if her body had taken on animalistic instincts. Danger lurked ahead of them, as well as behind. She felt it. She could almost smell death in the air, and though she was finding new powers every day—every hour—she still did not know who death had come for tonight.

Beyond the palace, the clock struck midnight. Thick stone walls muffled the sound, but it was distinct. Midnight was her time. *Their* time.

The bells announcing midnight were still pealing as she and Blade took the rear entrance to the gardens. The exit should have been guarded, but no sentinels stood watch there. A shiver made its way up Lyssa's spine. Sentinels should have been there. This was wrong. All wrong.

They stepped into the night, and Blade went still. So did Lyssa. He heard, as she did, whispers from the lush garden. Instead of turning in the other direction, he walked—cautiously, making little noise in the still night— along the garden path toward the whispers. Lyssa would have preferred a clean escape, but if Blade thought it was necessary that they move toward the voices instead of away from them, she would follow without question.

The empress's gardens were well kept and on a spring day a sight to behold. Flowers bloomed everywhere in abundance. No weed dared to grow here, and if it did it was immediately plucked out and discarded by one of an army of gardeners.

At night, the lush garden was deserted, but no less beautiful by moonlight and the occasional oil lamp that burned softly, even at this hour.

When they turned the corner and saw the scene ahead, Lyssa recoiled in horror. Three girls, pretty blondes, stood straight ahead. Two of them were in the process of wrapping their arms around two entranced sentinels. The third blonde stood back, well away from the romantic scene.

Perhaps outwardly the scene was romantic, but Lyssa saw monsters' faces on the two who looked so small and defenseless against the larger soldiers. She saw—and felt—darkness enveloping them. The third...the third, a slight young girl who stood with her back to them, was a mixture of darkness and light, and the war within her was causing her horrible pain. Like the other two, she wore a plain white shift not much longer than knee length, her fair hair loose, and no shoes. They all looked as if they'd just crawled from bed.

The sentinels were unaware that anyone watched; they had eyes only for the delicate-looking girls before them.

One girl latched her mouth to the lips of a sentinel. The other looked at Lyssa and Blade, and then at the third blonde, the uncertain one. The girl poised to kiss the entranced man said, "Kill them," and then she took her own sentinel into her arms.

Chapter Eighteen

Blade watched in horror as the sentinels were trapped in a killing embrace. He started to rush forward to try to save them, even though he realized it was too late. The men had already begun to shrink, to fade away. The girl who did not have a sentinel of her own to devour turned to face them after she was ordered to kill. Head down, she took a step forward but then she stopped. She lifted her head slowly, and Blade stopped, too. He did not even breathe.

Runa. Older, almost a woman, the very picture of the Runa he had seen in his fever dream…which had not been a dream or a glimpse into the Land of the Dead after all, apparently, but a visitation of some kind. For a moment everything else faded away. He held his breath and his knees went weak. Runa was alive. It was impossible, but she was right *there.* Judging by the expression on her face, she was not nearly as surprised to see him as he was to see her.

Outwardly the slight, young girl—his sister—looked to be no threat to anyone, but he knew her appearance was deceptive. They'd been apart so long, and she was no longer a child. She could be just like the others now. Was she the girl he remembered or was she a monster?

He'd tried so hard to protect her, to shield her from a world that would happily and self-righteously destroy her if they knew the secret of her birth. He'd loved her as a brother should; he'd told her again and again that her life—her soul—would be what she made it, not what anyone else declared it to be.

Had it been enough to save her when she'd been in this place, with these demons, for the past four years? He knew who she'd once been, but he did not know who—or what—she had become.

Lyssa tried to step around him, but he reached out, grabbing her, pulling her back. Runa took a few steps forward, short, tentative steps. "No," he said gruffly, holding onto Lyssa tightly, holding her in place. Dear God, was he going to be forced to choose between his wife and his sister?

"I can help her," Lyssa whispered. "Not the others, they are beyond saving, but…this one I can help."

"No one can help me," Runa whispered as she came closer.

"I can." Lyssa turned her head, she looked at Blade, caught his eye. "But there isn't much time. Trust me, as I trust you."

Trust me. He let her go, and she stepped in front of Runa.

"No one can help me," Runa said again. "I'm poison, inside and out. Don't touch me…."

Without warning, Lyssa did just that. She reached out and placed both hands on Runa's shoulders. Lyssa's body lurched and twitched, but she didn't let go. Her knees started to buckle, and Blade instinctively caught her. He started to pull her away, to yank her away from the danger she had brought upon herself, but she knew what he was thinking before he did and she whispered, "Not yet."

Runa closed her eyes and sighed. Tears ran down her face, and she sobbed.

And was that green light in Lyssa's hands an unnatural light she was transferring to Runa? It was magic, it was healing, it was such a big part of who Lyssa was; of who she had become. She shared it freely.

The three of them were one, for a long moment. Lyssa touched Runa; Blade held Lyssa. Past and present melded. Danced. Blade felt Lyssa's magic, her pain, and her determination to save this one girl—this one demon. He felt Runa's pain, too; not only the physical pain of this moment but of life. Of being different, of hiding who and what she was from everyone but him.

Blade had no magic. He was a simple man who had tried very hard to deny the existence of magic even when it had been right before him. But watching his sister and his wife, feeling what they felt…he could see the change on Runa's face, the shift in the way she held her body. Most sharply of all, he felt the tug of war between good and evil, dark and light.

The green light died; Lyssa dropped her hands and stepped back, all but falling into his arms. She was weak and needed his support, and he gave it to her.

Mere seconds had passed. Ahead the other two Ksanas continued to feed. It was too late to save the sentinels, had been too late from the moment the demons had captured their minds.

"Go, now," Lyssa said to Runa. "Run while you can."

Runa did not immediately do as she was told. She stepped toward them and smiled. "You are the witch, yes? Lyssa?"

Not so long ago he would have been alarmed that Runa knew his wife's name, but tonight nothing surprised him. He was beyond surprise.

Lyssa was not surprised, either. "I am."

"The witch and the blade." Runa smiled, and for an instant she was the little sister he remembered. Not a half-demon; just a girl. "I should have known all along it was you."

"Runa…"

Lyssa's head snapped around. "This is your—"

"Yes. Blade saved me long ago." Runa reached up, cupped his cheek with one soft hand. "He didn't know that was what he was doing, but…with love and kindness, he saved me."

He'd always thought he'd failed her, that he hadn't been fast enough….

"I will find you!" Runa dropped her hand and turned, running but barely making a sound, blending into the dark shadows of the garden and then disappearing. Straight ahead, there was not much left of the sentinels. They were literally skin and bones, their uniforms sagging, their weapons lying discarded on the ground.

"Ksana demons," Lyssa said. "Don't let their appearance fool you. Unlike Runa, those two are beyond saving, and they will not be easy to kill."

And he still did not have a sword.

A part of her wanted to take Blade's hand and pull him away. They should run, as Runa had, not confront. They should flee and hide, and protect their child and themselves at all costs.

But a stronger part of her knew this was why they had been brought together. This was why she had been denied the simple life she'd craved. They could not allow these Ksana demons to escape. *The witch and the blade.*

Unlike Runa, these two were completely dark. They were lost to the kind of magic that people like Edine feared so deeply that they would deny a lifelong friend. They were evil. The Ksana demons finished feeding upon the sentinels and dropped what was left of them to the ground, discarding clothing and dried carcasses as if they were tossing aside the bones of a roast chicken.

Having just consumed the life force of the two sentinels, the girls were strong, making them formidable opponents. And still…she and Blade could not run from this.

One girl stepped in front of the other and grinned. In that moment she did not look at all like a child. She was enveloped in darkness, a monster through and through. "I thought I'd like to feed on the blade, who by the way does not even have a sword, which is rather disappointing. But the witch looks as if she would provide a powerful nourishment."

She and the demon were two sides of the same coin, Lyssa realized. Life and death, healing and destruction. It was a terrifying thought, and at the same time…right. For every midnight there was a dawn. Lyssa knew she should be afraid, that she should be terrified to face these demons. But she was not. She was stronger than they were. They could not touch her….

Just as she had that thought, the girl in the lead lost her smile. Blade cursed as Lyssa moved forward without fear.

For a few moments the two Ksanas seemed to be transfixed. The cold fire Lyssa had felt in her hands on more than one occasion now shot through her entire body. Instead of being afraid, she welcomed that cold fire. It was hers. She *owned* it. Lyssa was surrounded by her witchy green light, coloring everything around her with that emerald haze. As the strength of that light grew stronger and brighter, Lyssa herself felt stronger. Brighter.

The demon to the rear began to back away, one step and then another, and Lyssa knew why. There was death for them in her light, and they saw it. Healing for humans, death for those with demon blood. She'd been able to touch and heal Runa, but only because there was light left within her.

The Ksanas were so fixated on the light that she realized they had lost sight of Blade. They had eyes only for her. She sensed Blade skirting around her to what was left of the sentinels. Hunkering low, he grabbed not one sword but two. With those weapons in his hands, he rose. Slowly. Determined. For a man who had never, as far as she knew, wielded a sword, he held them well.

The witch and the blade. Lyssa understood now. They were to be warriors in a war that had not yet begun. They were light to the dark, dawn to the moonless night of the demon daughters. So much for her ordinary life…

The Ksana to the rear, the one with hair so fair it was white in the moonlight, finally heard or saw or sensed Blade and spun around to face him. For a moment or two, she hummed a strange, off-key tune. For a fleeting moment, Lyssa could feel the girl's thoughts. The Ksana was not afraid. Not of a mere man, no matter what the prophecy said. After all, until now, swords and men had been of no danger to her. She was hard to kill, and all men fell under her spell. Blade hesitated, and Lyssa knew he was momentarily fooled by the Ksana's innocent appearance. She looked like any other young woman, slight and fragile, and in need of protection. But it was an illusion; a demon's trick.

There was only one way Lyssa knew of to make sure the demon would die and stay dead. She shouted, "Take her head!"

She'd never seen Blade handle a sword, and for a moment she worried that he might fumble or find the weight of the weapons to be awkward. Until he'd been hopelessly outnumbered, with only a dagger for a weapon he'd held his own against the men who'd abducted her on

Volker's orders. The swords were heavier, harder to control, though, and there was no time for him to practice.

Her worry didn't last long. Blade moved as if he'd been born with a sword in his hand, his motions fluid and strong. He wielded the swords as if they weighed nothing, as if they were extensions of his arms. And there was…no, she was not mistaken, there was an emerald green light dancing off the blades. Not her light, this time, but *his*. The demon with the silver hair danced out of the way, hummed a bit more, and then tried to move in. She even tried, Lyssa saw, to capture Blade with her eyes and hold him in place. But he was immune to her power, and that immunity confused her. He moved more quickly than any man should be able to as he swung one sword and severed the demon's head.

The other Ksana, the one who had been in the lead, spun around and screamed. "Divya! My sister!" She clasped both hands to her throat as if she felt the other demon's pain, and she screamed again, the sound piercing and inhuman in the night.

Blade turned his attention to the remaining Ksana. She did not wait for him to attack but leapt, her body all but flying through the air. She descended on him like an eagle swooping down to capture its prey. One of the swords Blade wielded pierced her belly, slicing through her body. It would have been a killing wound for any human, but the Ksana seemed not to feel any pain as she pushed away and freed herself, then twisted forward and grabbed Blade's hair. She tried to pull his mouth to hers but he resisted, and he continued to attack. His steel cut deeply into her, again piercing through her body, the bloodied blade exiting through her back once more…and still she wrestled with Blade, trying to impart her deadly kiss.

She was so close, he was in no position to take her head as he had taken her "sister's." He continued to fight, but if she managed to lay her mouth on him…

Lyssa ran toward the battle. Surely she could help, somehow. Would her touch be enough? Were her instincts about her magic bringing death to the demons correct, or had that been a moment of wishful thinking? She had to try…had to do something.

But before she could get close enough to do anything a strong hand stopped her, grabbing her hair and pulling her back. Her head snapped around; her feet slid out from under her. She scrambled for purchase so she could fight back but his grip kept her off balance. A sentinel? Another demon? Who had stopped her?

She wanted to scream, but could not. For a moment she could not even breathe. Blade pushed the Ksana away, forcing her off one sword while he swung the other. The Ksana jumped out of the way, trying to avoid the steel, but the tip of the blade cut deeply into her throat—inches deep. She held her damaged neck and backed away, furious and bloody, but still alive. She fell to the ground and crawled slowly into the shadows, injured but far from dead. Healing, Lyssa suspected, even as she made her escape.

Blade began to follow the demon, but the words—oh, that horrible *voice*—of the man holding Lyssa arrested him.

"Stop right there!"

Blade turned. Even in the night she could see him go pale. "Volker."

And then Lyssa felt the cold steel of a dagger at her own throat.

Chapter Nineteen

Blade swore silently as his personal demon held Lyssa's head twisted to the side so that the sharp edge of his dagger pressed against the vein in her slender throat. He forgot that the Ksana demon was crawling away, his focus narrowing to Lyssa. It should not be possible that the same man who'd driven steel into Runa would kill Lyssa, but that was a single twitch of a wrist from happening.

And if it did, Lyssa would not return from the dead as Runa had. Lyssa would die.

"Let her go," he said, wondering if either Lyssa or Volker could understand his rough words. They seemed to catch in his throat.

Volker peeked over Lyssa's head as he hid behind her, using her as a shield as he threatened her. Good. A dead shield would be of no use at all. "Do you have any idea how difficult it was to capture those three girls?"

One dead, one wounded, Runa...gone?

"Girls?" Blade's voice was sharper now, clearer. "They were not *girls*." None of them, not even his sister.

Volker shrugged. "Perhaps not in the purest sense of the word, but they were mine. I suppose any that were so easily disposed of wouldn't have done me much good in the long run. But there are others. An army, or what will soon be an army." Beyond the palace, a mournful wail rose. Volker's head snapped around; an unnatural chill made the hairs on the back of Blade's neck stand up. That howl was both human and not, and it was filled with pain. It echoed, the stuff of nightmares. "Did you hear that? Another of my girls, one of many you have not yet met."

Blade took a step forward, but Volker did not stay distracted long enough for him to move in.

"Who are you?" Volker asked as he pressed the blade more firmly against Lyssa's throat. "Why are you here? You must be the blade to this witch, the man who gives my girls nightmares. I thought you were dead." His eyes flitted to the swords Blade carried, swords stained with the blood of his *girls*.

The man did not know. Years of investigating and tracking and killing, and Miron Volker had no idea that all this time Blade had been searching for him.

"You took my sister," he said.

Volker sighed. "Is that all? I took many. I killed more. Men and women, young and old. Human and…not. I did what I had to do in order to shape this country into what it can and should be. Emperor Jahn is weak. What others see as kindness, I know to be weakness. He needs to be replaced."

"By you."

"By me," Volker agreed, tilting his head, narrowing his eyes. "I remember you now. Didn't I kill you once already?"

"You tried."

"Twice. First by my own hand and again at the hands of others. I sent my best men to do the job. What *are* you?"

"Just a man looking for justice."

Volker sighed. "Some families were relieved when I took their girls into my care. Who wants a demon sleeping in the next bed?"

Blade shook his head. "I thought you'd killed Runa, but she was here all along."

"The demons are hard to kill, I have found. Like you, apparently," Volker growled. "Some are harder to kill than others. There have been times when I've had to wound them severely in order to transport them here without incident. Your sister…"

"Runa. She has a name."

"Runa, then. She's a powerful one. I have given serious consideration to making her one of my empresses, when the time comes. Unless, of course, you've already killed her."

"No."

"Good. She'll return to me, then. She likes it here. She likes her place at my side. Your sister is not the sweet girl you imagine her to be. She's a pretty demon who drains the life from those she touches, and she grows stronger every day. If I had tried to take her *after* she'd come into her own, rather than identifying her early on, I never would have succeeded." Volker smiled. "She's killed far more men than I have."

Blade's vision narrowed. He could barely breathe. He'd always seen Runa as an innocent child, but in his heart he knew she was not. Was Volker lying now, attempting to make Blade doubt himself and his sister? Perhaps. It didn't matter. "If she killed, it was not her fault."

"If that makes you feel better, you can choose to believe it's so. But you're wrong. Your little sister is a bloodthirsty, murdering fiend. She is the stuff of nightmares."

Blade tightened his grip on the weapons he held and prepared to rush forward, but an unexpected voice in his head stopped him. *Be still. He's lying. He's hoping you'll make a rash move so he can kill us both.*

Lyssa's voice. And she was right.

The moment will come. Soon. Not yet.

Blade made an effort to keep his voice as steady as Volker's. "The men who were with you that day, I killed them…one after another. I hunted them down and slit their throats."

Volker was not so smug now, since his plan to incite Blade had failed. "They were soldiers in a coming war, and no soldier's life is without risk. At that time I was forced to use common mercenaries. I disguised them as sentinels, cleaned them up and gave them uniforms, but they obeyed me because I paid them. These days I have real soldiers, trained and dedicated men who will not be so easy to kill."

"If I kill you, those soldiers will have no one to command them."

"You won't kill me." Volker took a step back, dragging Lyssa with him, using her as a shield for as long as he needed her. Once they were out of sight, he would no longer have need of her. "Drop those swords or I'll cut her. Again. Deeper, this time. Not all wounds heal, not even for a witch with the gift of healing."

Instinct and fear for Lyssa commanded that Blade to do as Volker commanded, but he did not. Without these swords at the ready, they were both dead. He reminded himself that for now, Volker's fear kept Lyssa alive. That a dead shield was no good at all.

"Let her go," Blade said calmly. "When she's safe you can have the swords. And me."

Volker shook his head, then shouted, "Drop them now!"

Once again Blade heard Lyssa's voice, as clearly as if she were whispering in his ear.

Now.

He watched as, taking advantage of Volker's surge of emotion, Lyssa jabbed her elbow into the man's ribs and, when he reacted, twisted away from the knife and threw herself down. Blade watched as she hit the ground and a streak of blood bloomed on her throat. She'd been cut, but he did not know how badly or how deeply. He didn't slow down to tend to her; not yet. Instead he raised the sword in his right hand and swung it toward Miron Volker's head as Lyssa rolled away.

And the fight began. Volker drew his own sword as Blade swung his, knowing that, unlike Runa, Volker did not have the power to heal.

On her belly, low and bloody in the lushest part of the garden, Princess watched the two men fight. The man who had betrayed her and the blade. Which one did she hate more deeply? She held a hand to her almost severed throat, and tried to will the blood that flowed from her midsection to slow. But she was growing weaker by the moment. A human would be dead by now, but her demon blood, the blood she was spilling at an alarming rate, kept her alive.

The witch—Lyssa—rose slowly to her feet, her hand at her own injured throat. Her wound was small, insignificant compared to the gash that had almost taken Princess's head.

Volker had taken away her name and called her Princess, making her feel as if she were special, as if she were the *only one*. But Princess now knew that she was not the only one, not at all. She was one of many to him, no better than the expendable soldiers he talked about.

Had he been lying when he'd told the blade that he'd planned to make Runa an empress? *Runa?*

Volker had always painted such a pretty picture of power and wealth and love. A father's love, her sisters' devotion. But he only wanted that power for himself. She and her sisters were tools, nothing more.

They did not need him. She saw that now with crystal clarity. United, she and her sisters could take the power and wealth—and love—for themselves.

Blade fought with everything he had; for Lyssa, for Runa…for himself. He did not think, did not plan every move, step, swing or jab of a sword. Instead he fought with an instinct he had not known he possessed. With a sword in each hand he held his own, he battled a man that was as much a monster as those demons he called his girls.

Volker was well practiced with a sword, but he was afraid. He had never intended to do his own dirty work. Blade saw the fear in the minister's eyes. He swung with all his might and sliced Volker's shirt and the skin beneath. Blood bloomed and Volker screamed—not in pain but in fury that he had been injured.

Blade understood very well that he was not protected; that he could be killed. If death came fast enough, not even Lyssa could save him. And as he fought, he also realized that he did not want to die. After years of not caring if justice cost him his life, he wanted to live. A life with Lyssa awaited him when this was done. His life was so much more than delivering justice to one man. So much more than avenging Runa.

Without warning Volker feinted to the side, stepped and turned, then swung his sword. Blade jumped back, and the tip of the sword scratched his arm. It was a deep scratch, but far from the killing blow his opponent had intended. And Blade responded with a swing of his own sword.

♦ ♦ ♦

From her position low in the garden, Princess watched. If she could take in the life force of another she would be able to heal quickly. If she had not already fed well tonight, she would be truly dead, like Divya.

Princess mourned the loss of her sister. Divya had been silly and selfish on occasion, but she'd also been a part of the whole; a sister by blood and by bond. Runa was gone, too, but not in the same way. She lived, but she was no longer a part of the whole as she had once been. Her connection to her sisters—imperfect as it had been—had been broken by the witch. Runa would never be the same. She was no longer demon, but neither was she human. She would have nowhere to go, no one to call her own. No family. No place in the world.

She would certainly never be an empress.

Princess needed desperately to feed, and for a moment she considered that while the men fought she could take the witch by surprise, but knowing what Lyssa had done to Runa, Princess was afraid to touch her, especially in her weakened state. Did the witch have the power to strip away the demon? That green light was terrifying; it was death to her and her sisters. Was that why she and the others had been warned? There was more than one kind of death, and the idea of being permanently separated from her sisters, to have that connection stripped away…a true death was preferable.

Volker and the blade were evenly matched. Their swords met as they danced on the pathway and into the gardens. Each was wounded, but neither had fallen. Not yet.

Lyssa's head snapped around; Princess heard what she heard. Several sentinels were coming, and quickly. Boots in the near distance; shouts, one soldier to another. The witch offered a sharp warning to her man. Volker faltered; and the blade took advantage of the lapse and ran his sword through the man Princess had sworn never to call Father again.

Minister Volker fell, half on the path, half in the garden. He destroyed flowers as he landed, and soft petals dropped onto his back and into his hair. Princess had the fleeting thought that she should be sad, that she should cry for him, but she did not. Perhaps she had called him Father, for a while, but no more. The witch Lyssa took her man's hand, and they ran toward the rear palace wall, away from the approaching sentinels. In moments those sentinels would find their wounded minister. She had to act quickly, before they took him away.

Princess crawled toward Volker. Her bloody hand touched his, and with the last of her strength she pulled him toward her, off the path, into the shadows. Her lips hovered over his as his eyes opened. She could see his thoughts, feel his hope. Oh, how sweet. He believed she was going to save him, even now.

"Father?" she whispered. "I need you." And then she placed her mouth on his before he had the chance to scream.

Chapter Twenty

They didn't have much time, but Lyssa knew better than to run without preparation. This time she would have food, blankets, and a weapon of her own. And she would deliver a proper goodbye to her father. She didn't know when, or if, she would return to Arthes.

Everyone would soon realize that she and Blade had been the ones to spill blood in Empress Morgana's beautiful garden. Blade had lied to the physician and they'd escaped...what other logical conclusion could anyone come to? And if Volker survived this night, what kind of tale would he spin? Not a pretty one, she imagined.

They had work to do, a war to fight, and they would not begin it by running blindly into the forest with no preparation.

Though the forest was calling...whispering...singing...

Lyssa was certain she would have to bang on the door of her home in order to wake her father and Sinmora, but when she turned the corner of her street she saw them there, standing in front of the open door looking puzzled. Her father carried a lantern that caught the two of them in a circle of soft light, a beacon calling Lyssa home.

And they were not alone. Edine was there, just behind them. Without her children, without her husband. She carried a small cloth-wrapped parcel in her hand, and had leaned forward to whisper to Cyrus Tempest.

At once, all three became aware that Lyssa and Blade were approaching. They turned, stopped talking, and waited.

Lyssa could not take her eyes from Edine, who spoke first, as she took a long step forward to meet her…friend? Yes, friends still. Always.

"I had a dream…you were there and you were hurt, and you needed me and it was all so real, and I…Oh, Lyssa, I'm so sorry."

Lyssa hugged her friend and felt a great rush of relief. Yes, friends always. No matter what.

"I was scared," Edine said. "And such a fool! Forgive me. I do love you."

"Of course I forgive you. I love you, too." Lyssa stepped away from her friend. Tempting as it was, there was no time to linger here.

"Bread and dried meat," Edine said as she handed over the cloth-wrapped package she'd been carrying. "I don't know why, but when I woke from my dream I knew I had to come here, and I knew you would need this. Maybe I possess a little bit of magic myself."

"I am positively starving," Lyssa confessed. "We'll make good use of this very soon."

"I dreamed of you, too," Sinmora whispered. "It was…horrid."

"Unlike the ladies, I could not sleep at all," her Papa added, "not after seeing you…hurt." He shook his head. "My beloved daughter…I have been a terrible father. I love you dearly. Please don't ever doubt that, and I did try…But there are so many things I should have told you, so many…."

"You were a wonderful father," Lyssa said. "And you will be a wonderful father again."

"How did you know? I…we…Never mind. I have so much to tell you, there's so much I should have said long ago."

Time was short, and she knew it, but she could not leave so much unsaid. "I was angry with you for not telling me about the baby, and then—not so long ago—I realized that I was just as much at fault because I did not tell you that I had overheard you and Sinmora talking about the baby. One kept secret does not make another right."

Blade stepped forward. He still carried both swords, and his clothes—fancy as they were—were stained with blood, some of it his, most of it not. By moonlight and the one lantern her father carried, he was a frightful sight. This was the primitive man she'd first seen on the street, the man who'd rescued her from the tavern as midnight approached.

But no one was afraid of him. They all saw in him what she saw. He was hers and would protect her always.

"This is all very well and good," Blade said sharply, "but we have no time for sentiment, much less conversations that should have been held years ago. Another time, perhaps. Right now we need blankets, a flint, food, and a water skin. We both need a change of clothes, and Lyssa will require a warm cloak."

"And you?" Cyrus asked. "What else do you need?"

Blade hesitated for a moment. "Deliver a message to Hagan Elmar, if you will. Tell him…tell him it's done."

"That's all? It's done?"

"Tell him I found the man I was looking for and…tell him Runa lives," Blade added in a lowered voice.

So much to be done, so little time…Blade's words about a message spurred Lyssa to speak up. "You must tell Empress Morgana that the emperor has enemies all around him. His Foreign Minister is a traitor. I doubt Volker will survive the night, but if he does, Emperor Jahn needs to be warned. Even if Volker dies, there are others." He had not been working alone.

"She might not believe me," her father began.

"Make her believe," Lyssa said sharply.

They gathered all they needed, all they could carry, and Lyssa enjoyed a last round of hugs. There were tears, but none of them were hers. As she and Blade headed away from the center of town, toward the forest, they heard a cry of alarm from the palace.

And they ran.

Blade carried the swords he'd taken from the sentinels who'd died at the hands of Ksana demons—now also dead—in scabbards that hung at his back. They each carried a large canvas sack of supplies; enough for a few days, at least.

Soon the woods swallowed them whole. Even though they could not see what lay before them, they moved quickly and easily, as if they were being guided to safety by unseen hands. Instinctively they leapt over fallen logs and around low lying bushes. Once, in the distance, Lyssa saw the glowing eyes of an animal, but it only watched and let them be. She was not afraid, even though she remembered all too clearly that chilling howl and wondered—for a moment—if those eyes were indeed those of an ordinary animal.

They were deep in the woods before she stopped to take a deep breath and look Blade up and down. They'd left in such a hurry! She was starving, and she was tired. Even though they had tried to prepare, there was so much to be said, still so much to be done. It occurred to her that she should have asked her father for bandages.

Oh, wait, she didn't need bandages. She could heal every cut on Blade's body, every scrape, with a touch.

He took her in his arms and pulled her close. It was nice; it was beautiful. She hid her face against his chest and listened to his heartbeat.

"I'm sorry," he said. "I didn't want this for you. I never meant to make you a part of my revenge." He barely paused before he asked, "How is your throat?"

"Healed." Completely. As soon as she washed the blood from her skin, there would be no sign that she'd ever been cut. "When I can see you more clearly I'll take care of your wounds, as well."

"No," he whispered. "None are life threatening. They will heal on their own, in time."

Her heart sank. They were meant to be together, they had a tremendous job ahead of them...but that didn't mean Blade would love her; that didn't mean they would be more than soldiers on the same side in a battle between good and evil. There were moments when she knew without doubt that he cared for her, that she was convinced he was hers in an elemental way. But then there were other moments when she doubted everything.

"Are you afraid of me?" she asked. "Afraid to let me touch you?" She was touching him now, as he held her so close, but not with magic. And that magic was such a part of who she was. What she was.

Her healing touch didn't just affect him physically, it also touched his soul. It changed him, and maybe he didn't want to be changed any more.

"No. But I waited a very long time to face Miron Volker. I don't mind carrying the reminders of that encounter for a while longer."

"If you change your mind..."

He leaned down and kissed her. It was a deep, stirring, important kiss. His lips molded to hers; their tongues danced. No, he was not afraid to touch her, not like this.

Lyssa got lost in the kiss; she let it feed her. There was power in a kiss. The Ksana demons used a kiss to kill, to take life's force. A kiss fed Lyssa, too, but there was a difference. She didn't take life…she could give it. Could her kiss alone heal Blade? Did he crave her the way she craved him, or was she simply an obligation?

Again she had the thought that the two of them and the demon daughters were two sides of the same coin. Light and dark, love and hate, good and evil.

Blade was hers, in so many ways. She was his. And she so wanted them—together—to be more than soldiers on the same side of the fight.

"What now?" she asked, when he ended the kiss.

"We find Runa, or else we let her find us. She's close, I can feel it."

Yes, she *was* close. Lyssa felt it, too. "All right."

"There are more like them, Lyssa. There are so many more demon daughters. You heard that howl. You saw the expression on Volker's face when he talked about all his *girls*. A part of me wants to hide you away and protect you from everything, even from my sister, but…"

"But that's not what we're meant for, is it?"

"No, that's not what we're meant for."

Some, like Runa, could be saved. Others, like the two blondes who had devoured the sentinels, could not. They were pretty monsters, but they were indeed monsters.

Lyssa put her hands on Blade's face. "We will find your sister, and we will care for her. We will make her a part of our family."

"It will be dangerous, though I don't really have any idea *how* dangerous."

He pulled her close once more, and she was happy to rest her head against his chest again. A couple of tears fell, soaking into his shirt, but she did not sob. He would wonder why. The reason for her tears was simple, but she could not share this truth.

She wanted him to love her, so much.

Soon she would tell him about the baby, their daughter. But not now. Not like this. She would share the news in the sunlight, with a smile on her face and no tears stinging her eyes. No matter how he might feel about her, he would love his daughter. Wouldn't he?

Yes. The knowing came the way it sometimes did, and she wondered if she would ever be powerful enough to have all the answers. She hoped not. It would be…exhausting.

"I love you," Blade said as he tightened his hold on her. "Not because of a prophecy, not because you've touched me inside and out with your magic. And your body," he added, almost teasing. "It's deeper than that. It's more. I was meant for you, Lyssa, and you were meant for me. Even if we do have demons to fight and sentinels to avoid, even if our life is anything but ordinary…I love you."

Connected by magic or not, she knew he spoke the truth. His words dried her tears. They were one. *More.* They were joined in spirit and always would be. The man she loved, her Blade, made her so much more than she'd ever imagined she could be.

"Thank you," she whispered.

He drew away, a little, and looked down at her. "Thank you?"

She gripped his jacket, held on tight. "I wondered, not too long ago, if I should thank you or curse you for showing me, for *teaching* me, what love and true marriage is like. I have decided to thank you."

It was hard to tell, in the darkness, but she thought he gave in to a smile.

I love you, too, more than you will ever know. She thought the words, and Blade heard them. And then she said the words aloud, because she could. "I love you."

An ordinary life?

Never.

The End

Recent releases

Running Wild, Ballantine, written with Linda Howard
A Week Till the Wedding, Harlequin Special Edition

Previous Columbyana books

The Sun Witch
The Moon Witch
The Star Witch

Prince of Magic
Prince of Fire
Prince of Swords

Untouchable
22 Nights
Bride by Command

For a complete list of previous releases, visit
www.lindawinsteadjones.com

Linda Winstead Jones

Linda's first book, the historical romance *Guardian Angel*, was released in 1994, and in the years since she's written in several romance sub-genres under several names. In order of appearance, Linda Winstead; Linda Jones; Linda Winstead Jones; Linda Devlin; and Linda Fallon. She's a six time finalist for the RITA Award and a winner (for *Shades of Midnight*, writing as Linda Fallon) in the paranormal category. Most recently she's been writing as Linda Jones in a couple of joint projects with Linda Howard, and rereleasing some of her backlist in ebook format. She can be found at any one of a variety of Facebook pages (search for Linda Winstead Jones and Linda Howard/Linda Jones) and at: **www.lindawinsteadjones.com**.

Linda lives in Huntsville, Alabama. She can be reached at…

E-mail:
lindawinsteadjonesauthor@gmail.com

Twitter at @LWJbooks
https://twitter.com/LWJbooks

Facebook:
https://www.facebook.com/pages/Linda-Winstead-Jones/103936415079